Let's go

得文化
Culture

U0077354

好學
用的

Smart
網購英文

英對照輕鬆GO!!! 迅速掌握購物要訣!!!

Jessica Su ◎ 著

uyers 要學 Sellers 更要知道的網購經

MART 網購 3 大特色 ➡ 晉升聰明消費高手

網購教學篇
教學篇12個Instructions：
熟悉介面、挑對網路店家 ➡ 操作、付款樣樣行
了解Paypal、關稅和運費 ➡ 精打細算網購專家!!!

網購商品篇
商品篇12個Choices ➡ 時尚品牌、休閒服飾、
嬰兒週邊商品百百款
購買國外折扣精品 ➡ 貨比三家真划算!!!

網購旅遊篇
旅遊篇10個Places ➡ 收集資料 (EX飯店、機票) 不可少
遊樂園、海生館和博物館 GOGOGO ➡ 交通行程好順暢!!!

Preface 作者序

　　網際網路興起大大的改變了人們購物習慣。面對滿是英文國外購物網站與旅遊網站，您是否心動，卻因不知該如何下手而苦惱？

　　【教學篇】本書海外購物網站教學篇，一步步教您從國外網站註冊、商品挑選、看懂國外網站尺寸、運費規則，安排運送方式等。讓您慢慢看懂國際網路購物流程。

　　【商品篇】列出時下最受歡迎的相關網站介紹，不論您是愛運動的學生，追求時尚的上班族，愛打扮的小資女，或是顧家的好媽媽。都能在相關網站裡找到您所需要的商品，享受無價差的最新國際商品。

　　【旅遊篇】要告訴您如何規劃自助旅遊，有機票、飯店、到歐洲的火車訂票。本書能教您如何善用各類網站，為您的生活帶來更多美好的經驗。

Jessica Su

Editor 編者序

在食、衣、住、行、育、樂都脫離不了網購的時代，面對著消費習慣的改變我們不管是否抗拒，也漸漸熟悉了網購這個名詞，瞭解網購，甚至開始網購，就如同當初許多抗拒著使用智慧型手機的使用者一般，在瞭解後就愛不釋手了，但在未熟悉之前，面對著許多操作介面等，許多人常有的想法就像購買物品時，回應推銷員的那句：「怕買了不會操作，怕買了不會使用浪費了！」。好消息是，這本網購書籍規劃了三大篇章【教學篇】、【商品篇】和【旅遊篇】，閱讀後必能發現網購不但不煩人，介面也能輕鬆操作，從此體驗網購樂趣喔！

編輯部敬上

目次

Contents

Part 1 教學篇

目次
Contents

Part 3　旅遊篇

Part 1

教學篇

先註冊準沒錯

📺 網頁註冊篇

　　越來越多的海外網站瞄準了國際線上購物商機，紛紛推出了免運費的服務，只要達到一定的消費金額就能享有全球免運的服務。如此一來，網路購物變得更加便利及划算了！！要購物前，請先註冊吧！！

💎 情境對話

April: Meredith, you won't believe this .My sister is getting married.

Meredith，你知道嗎？我妹妹要結婚了。

Meredith: That sounds good news, <u>why the long face</u>.

聽起來是個好消息，你為什麼不開心呢？

April: <u>Don't get me wrong</u>. Of course, I'm happy for my sister. She has finally found somebody. But it's such an unexpected announcement.

別誤會，當然我很為她開心，她終於找到喜歡的人了。但是這消息有點讓人意外，我的衣服都太休閒

All my dresses are too casual. These are not appropriate for wedding.

了，穿去婚禮很不得體。

Meredith: What kind of dress you are looking for?

你想找什麼款式的洋裝呢？

April: Wrap dress, it's elegant and sexy, perfect for the wedding. However, it's quite time-consuming to get a wrap dress here.

V 領包覆式洋裝，那種看起來既優雅又很性感，穿去婚禮剛好。但是在這裡要找件 V 領包覆式洋裝要花好多時間。

Meredith: Can't agree with you anymore. Hey, have you tried Internet? There are a lot of beautiful dresses on Internet. Such as ASOS, BCBG and Forever 21.

十分同意你的話呀，嘿！你試過網路購物嗎？網路上有許多好看的洋裝像是 Asos、BCBG 及 Forever 21。

April: I never thought about it. But, the international freight is very expensive.

從來沒有想過，國際運費不是很貴嗎？

Meredith: There are more and more people shopping online. To follow this trend, more and more websites

越來越多人在網路上購物，為了因應這趨勢，也越來越多網站推出了免運

launch free-freight service if your order exceeds a certain amount.

費服務，只要你的訂單達到一定金額就可免運哦。

April: Really? That sounds very economical. But I never shop on an overseas website.

真的嗎？聽起來滿划算的！但是我沒有在國外網站上購物過。

Meredith: Don't worry. It's quite easy. I'll show you how. First, let's register on the shopping website.

別擔心，還滿簡單的，我會告訴你該怎麼做。首先，先在網站上註冊

April: Wow!! There are so many dresses online. I am sure that I can find some dresses there.

哇，網路上有好多漂亮的洋裝哦，我一定能找到喜歡的。

單字解析

Unexpected [ˌʌnɪkˈspɛktɪd] *adj.* 無法預知的
例 Jack is surprised by Kevin's unexpected visiting. They haven't seen each other for 10 years.
➜ 對於 Kevin 忽然來訪，Jack 感到很驚奇。他們已經 10 年沒見面了。

Announcement [əˈnaʊnsmənt] *n.* 聲明
例 The President made a dramatic announcement that united

the nation.

➜ 總統發表一個激勵人心的演講，使國家團結起來。

Appropriate [əˋproprɪˌet] *adj.* 適合的

例 For the Chinese custom, it's not appropriate to wear a black dress in the wedding.

➜ 以中國習俗來說，婚禮上穿著黑色洋裝不太適合。

Launch [lɔntʃ] *v.* 推出

例 The company will launch 10 bags this season.

➜ 該公司本季會推出 10 款新包。

Exceed [ɪkˋsid] *v.* 超過

例 Be careful. Don't drive exceed the speed limit.

➜ 小心！ 別超速了。

Register [ˋrɛdʒɪstɚ] *v.* /*n.* 註冊 登記

例 Many applicants came to register for the job interview.

➜ 許多申請人來登記工作面試。

句型解析

本書生活化的對話中為您介紹實用的句型或是短句，再舉例句說明，讓您看完之後，就能馬上輕鬆學會，不用背誦！！

Part 1 教學篇

Part 2 商品篇

Part 3 旅遊篇

Why the long face 怎麼看起來不開心

解 這裡的 long face 就是我們中文裡講的拉長臉，板著臉的意思

例 Don't pull the long face. Cheer up.

→ 不要板著臉，開心點 ！

Don't get me wrong 不要誤會我，沒有別的意思

解 通常，我們在建議別人時，或是表達意見之後。會加這句 Don't get me wrong.表示我們只是善意的提出意見，並沒有批評或是攻擊的意思。

例 Your proposal is quite impressive, don't get me wrong, but I think you should be more careful on spelling

→ 你的提案讓人印象深刻，我沒有別的意思，但是你的拼字要再加強。

以上的單字及短句十分的簡單與實用，
讓您購物之餘，也能自然而然的學習英文哦。

網頁註冊教學

▶▶▶ **Join** 加入網站

→ 以 **TOPSHOP** 網站為例 （圖片來源: https://www.topshop.com）

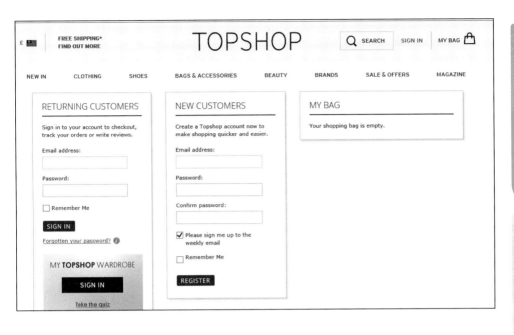

填入說明

Returning Customers　舊客戶登入

- Email address :填入自己郵件
- Password :填入密碼

New Customers　新客戶註冊

- Email address :填入自己郵件
- Password :填入密碼
- Confirm password: 確認密碼

Register 註冊（填好，請按此）

- 進入我的帳號

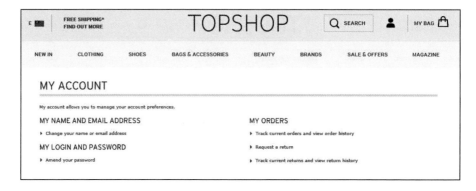

▶▶▶ 簡單註冊完成！！

➡ 以 **New Look** 網站為例 （圖片來源: https://www.newlook.com）

📝 填入說明

First Name: 填名字 Last Name: 填姓氏 Email address:電子信箱

- Date of Birth: 出生年月日（日，月，西元年）
- Contact telephone：連絡電話（台灣國碼 886 + 區碼+電話號碼，區碼不加 0）
- Mobile telephone：手機號碼（台灣國碼 886 + 手機號碼，手機號碼不加 0）
- Student number：學生號碼（英國學生證號碼，沒有免填）
- Password：密碼
- Confirm password：確認密碼

Register 註冊（填好，請按此）

- 註冊完成！！進入我的帳號

▶▶ 建立個人資料

➡ 以 **New Look** 網站為例 （圖片來源: https://www.newlook.com）

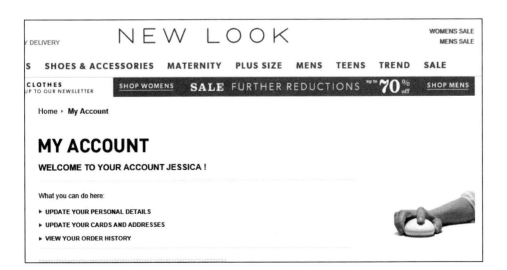

Part **1** 教學篇

Part **2** 商品篇

Part **3** 旅遊篇

網頁說明　我的帳號裡可以看到有三個選項

> UPDATE YOUR PERSONAL DETAILS　更新個人資料
> UPDATE YOUR CARDS AND ADDRESSES　更新信用卡及地址
> VIEW YOUR ORDER HISTORY　查看歷史訂單

NEW LOOK

DELIVERY

S　SHOES & ACCESSORIES　MATERNITY　PLUS SIZE　MENS　TEENS　TI

CLOTHES
P TO OUR NEWSLETTER　　SHOP WOMENS　SALE FURTHER REDUCTIONS

Home ▸ My Account ▸ My Addresses ▸ **Add a New Address**

ADD A NEW ADDRESS

Simply fill in the details for your new address below.
When you're done, you'll return to My address & Cards, and your new address will be saved.

ADDRESS DETAILS　　　　　　　　　　　　　　　　　　　　* Indicates a required field

First name*

Last name*

Country*　　　United Kingdom ▾

Postcode*　　　　　　　　　FIND ADDRESS ▸

Address line 1*

Address line 2

Address line 3

Town or city*

County

ADD THIS ADDRESS →

填寫說明

有關地址及信用卡資料填寫，請參考英文地址篇&信用卡篇。

❤ 小貼士

➤ 註冊完成時，通常您的信箱會收到網站寄來的歡迎信件。有些網站會在註冊完成時送給會員註冊禮，**如 Register to get 15% off coupon 註冊即得 15% 折價券**。而這折價券則會和網站的歡迎信件一併寄達。 如下：

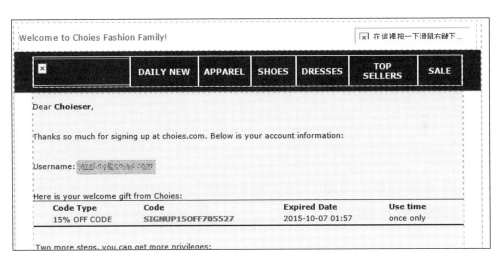

```
Welcome to Choies Fashion Family!                      [x] 在這裡按一下滑鼠右鍵下...

[x]      DAILY NEW   APPAREL   SHOES   DRESSES   TOP       SALE
                                                 SELLERS

Dear Choieser,

Thanks so much for signing up at choies.com. Below is your account information:

Username: 

Here is your welcome gift from Choies:
  Code Type        Code                  Expired Date        Use time
  15% OFF CODE     SIGNUP15OFF705527     2015-10-07 01:57    once only

Two more steps, you can get more privileges:
```

　　所以一旦完成註冊之後，請先到信箱查看哦。若有折價券的話就可即刻使用了。

➤ 現在的購物網站操作介面越來越簡單，如 Topshop 為例，只要填寫 email 帳號跟密碼，即完成簡單的註冊。您可以先完成這簡單的註冊，之後便會收到網站寄來的各式各樣的折扣訊息。

Part 1 教學篇

Part 2 商品篇

Part 3 旅遊篇

 英文地址篇

　　國外網購第一步，請先知道自家英文地址。除了收件地址之外，許多網站為確保個人資料的正確性及完整性，亦會要求輸入帳單地址。本篇要告訴您出現這些網頁時，該怎麼填寫。

情境對話

April: Meredith, after the registration, what should I do next?

Meredith，註冊完之後，接下來該怎麼辦呢？

Meredith: I suggest that you fill in the address detail in your account, such as billing address, delivery address. It will be more efficient for your online shopping.

我建議你可以將你帳號的資料建立起來，像是帳單地址，寄件地址等。這樣購物會比較便捷。

April: Why do they need my billing

為什麼網站需要我的帳單

address? Do I have one？

地址？我有帳單地址嗎？

Meredith: It's a secure procedure, to ensure that you are the credit card holder. As you know, more and more people shop online, the Internet security is always the first priority. Of course, you have billing address, you must fill it in when you applied for the credit card.

這只是個安全的程序，確定你是信用卡的持卡人。你知道越來越多的人使用網路購物，因此網路安全是首要考量。你當然有帳單地址，你以前申請信用卡的時候一定要填的。

April: Oh ～ that address. You reminded me. It's my mom's address.

哦，那個地址。你這一說，我想起來了，是我媽媽家的地址。

Meredith: Now you remember. Go to the post office website, they have free Chinese address translation service. It's quite convenient.

想起來了吧！郵局的網站，有免費的中文地址翻譯英文，十分簡單！

April: Ok, I filled in the billing address, next the delivery address.

我填好了帳單地址，現在要填寄送地址。

Meredith: Well, you should write your apartment address. Then you

嗯，為了及時收到包裹，你應該寫你住的公寓地

can receive the parcel in time.

址。

April: Exactly, anyway my mom won't need my V wrap dress.

說得對極了！反正我媽媽不需要 V 領洋裝啦！

Meredith: Ha ,very funny. <u>Remember to</u> write down your cell phone no., in case the carrier may have to contact you.

哈！很搞笑~記得要寫你的手機電話，以免快遞公司臨時要聯絡你。

April: Sure, will do. Thanks .

知道了，謝謝你呦。

 單字解析

Fill in [fɪl IN] 填寫

例 You must fill in the application before interview.

➡ 面試前你必須將申請表填寫完畢。

句型解析

 本書生活化的對話中為您介紹實用的句型或是短句，再舉例句說明，讓您看完之後，就能馬上輕鬆學會，不用背誦！！

S+ suggest that 某人建議

例 The rain is getting heavily. I suggest that you should stay .

➡ 雨越下越大，我建議你應該先留下。

例 The traffic is so bad, I suggest that you can make a detour.

➡ 交通實在太糟了，我建議你們可以繞路。

Remember to　記得要

解 這是個善意的提醒別人要記得去完成某事。

例 Remember to brush your teeth before school

➡ 上學前要記得刷牙。

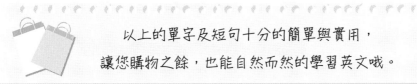

以上的單字及短句十分的簡單與實用，
讓您購物之餘，也能自然而然的學習英文哦。

💎 地址查詢與填寫

➡ **中華郵政地址中譯英** （其實查詢英文地址非常容易的，只要至郵局網站網址 http://www.post.gov.c/post/internet/Postal/index.jsp?ID=207）

輸入欲查詢的中文地址之後，按查詢。下方即會出現地址中翻英

➡ 填寫帳單地址

此項資料要跟您的**信用卡帳單地址**相符

First Name：名字　　Last Name：姓氏

Telephone Daytime：白天聯絡電話（台灣國碼為　+886）

Telephone Evening：晚上聯絡電話（台灣國碼為　+886）

Mobile：手機（台灣國碼為　+886）

Country：國家

Address：地址（請查詢中華郵政地址中譯英）

注意英文的地址表達方式跟中文剛好相反，是從幾號開始寫起的

City：城市

Postcode：郵遞區號

Optional：在此表示該欄位可填可不填

➡ 填寫送貨地址

送貨地址請填寫您想要貨物送達的地址，填寫方式與帳單地址相同。

➢ 請注意，為了交易安全，有些較謹慎的網站不接受帳單地址與送貨地址不相同。有些網站則是在下訂單確認時，請顧客勾選帳單地址與送貨地址不是同一個即可繼續操作。

➡ 關於網站的運送規定

Standard Shipping

Your order may be delivered to you by either the local post office or a local courier. Depending on your area, most orders will be delivered by your local post service, so the package will be received with your regular mail. If you are not home when the delivery is made, a notice card may be left by the postal service to advise on how and where your delivery can be collected.

Express Shipping

Your order will be delivered by UPS who will attempt to deliver the goods to you three (3) times. They will also leave a notice card after each delivery attempt to advise you what you can do to arrange the receipt of your package. Your signature will be required upon delivery.

➡ **中譯：**

標準運送：訂單會由當地郵局或是貨運運送，看地區而異。但是大部分會郵局運送，如同一般收信的方式送達。若剛好沒有人在，郵局可能會留下字條，告知如何領取包裹。

快遞運送：會由 UPS 投遞 3 次，若剛好沒有人在，UPS 也在每次投遞無人領取後，留下聯絡方式。包裹送達時必須簽收。

➡ **解析：一般來說，國際運送分為 2 種**

標準運送：走郵務系統的，從國外的郵局，送到台灣郵局或貨運。標準運送的運送時間較長，也沒有追蹤單號。通常免運的服務，多採標準運送。

快遞運送：就是像 UPS、DHL、Fedex 等國際快遞公司。從國外的人快遞運送送到台灣的 UPS 去投遞，快遞公司的運送時間短，較快，有追蹤單號可以查詢運送狀況，運費較高。

小貼士

➢ 填寫英文地址時，力求詳盡與清楚，這樣包裹送錯的機率才能降低。遞區號尤其重要，這樣包裹才能快速送達。

　此外，國際網站通常配合快遞公司送件，若是包裹在過海關時，有抽驗到，而需要支付關稅時。快遞公司會馬上與收件人聯繫。這時清楚的聯繫電話就很重要。所以請好好填寫資料吧！！

➢ 若你購買的商品是透過代運公司運送，請記得變更寄送地址，將寄送地址變更為代運公司所提供的美國境內地址。

Word Bank

Standard Shipping	標準運送	Post office	郵局
Local courier	當地貨運	Receive	收到
Regular mail	一般信件	Express Shipping	快遞運送
Notice	通知	Signature	簽名
Package	包裹		

尺寸該怎麼看

📺 尺寸篇

　　網購除了挑選喜歡的商品款式之外，最重要的就是確認尺寸。因為尺寸不合往往是退貨的主要原因，因此在您挑選商品時，花越多時間研究尺寸，越能避免退貨的情況發生。

💎 情境對話

April：Meredith, I received an email from Australia, All Metal industry, an agriculture tooling company. They requested about the wheelbarrow, and the order quantity is huge.

我收到一封澳洲來的詢價單，All Metal 工業，一家農具公司。他們想知道獨輪車的報價，而且數量不少。

Meredith: Forward the mail to me. I would like to read it.

把信轉寄給我，我來看看。

April：Sure, I am right on it !!

沒問題，馬上處理。

Meredith: April, I finished the wheel-barrow quotation and already sent an email to Mr. Avery, the general manager of All Metal Industry, If there is any further news, please keep me informed.

April，獨輪車的報價單已經完成了，我已經傳給 All Metal 工業的總經理 Mr.Avery 了。如果有任何消息，讓我知道。

April: Actually, their reply just came in. They requested 2 free samples.

事實上，他們剛傳來了回覆，要求 2 個樣品。

Meredith: Well, we can arrange the samples. Make sure to send the samples today via DHL. This potential client is important.

樣品可以給他，你今天用 DHL 將樣品寄出，這個客戶十分有潛力，很重要的。

April: Completely understand. I'll offer the tracking no. to Mr. Avery.

了解，寄出之後，我會將快遞單號給 Mr.Avery。

Meredith: Yes, it's the protocol. After the express delivery, we have to notify our client immediately. Why are you wearing this? It's kind of over-size.

沒錯，公司規定如此，快遞寄出之後，我們必須立刻通知客戶。為什麼你穿這個，好像有點大。

April: I know, I bought this online.

我知道，我在網路上購買

Part 1 教學篇

Part 2 商品篇

Part 3 旅遊篇

Normally, I'm size M in Taiwan, so I picked up a size M coat online. Obviously, I should read the size chart before placing the order.

的。因為在台灣我都是買 M 號的，所以我在網路上也是選 M 號，早知道下單前我應該先看清楚尺寸表。

Meredith: Why didn't you return it？

那你為什麼不退貨呢？

April: No, I really like this coat. Besides, the winter is coming. I could use a bigger coat.

不要了，我真的滿喜歡這外套的，而且冬天到了，大一點的外套比較好。

 單字解析

Forward [`fɔrwɚd] *v.* 轉寄
例 Don't forward Jo's mail to me. I'm not interested in his private life.
→ 不要把 Jo 的信轉寄給我，我對他的私生活沒有興趣。

Quotation [kwoˋteʃən] *n.* 報價單
例 Mr. Avery is satisfied with the wheelbarrow quotation.
→ Avery 先生對獨輪車的報價單十分滿意。

句型解析

本書生活化的對話中為您介紹實用的句型或是短句，再舉例句說明，讓您看完之後，就能馬上輕鬆學會，不用背誦!!

keep me informed 讓我隨時知道最新狀況

解 inform 是通知。Keep me informed 字面意思是保持通知我，就是有最新消息隨時回報

例 A: We already took your dog to the vet. You just wait here.

B: Thank you, please keep me informed

➡ A: 我們已經將你的狗帶去獸醫那了，你就在這等著。

B: 謝謝，有任何消息請通知我。

Kind of 有點

解 1.：這麼簡短的短句，看起來很簡單，其實用途很多。對於對方的問題含糊應對，不願正面回答。

例 A: Do you like an apple pie? Carl bought some apple pies.

B: well, kind of.

➡ A: 你喜歡蘋果派嗎?Carl 帶了一些蘋果派。

B: 恩，還好耶。

解 2.：用不確定的語氣，帶有修飾之意，有點～

例 I kind of feel sorry for him. It's not his fault.

➡ 我有點替他覺得可惜，這不是他的錯。

Part 1 教學篇

Part 2 商品篇

Part 3 旅遊篇

以上的單字及短句十分的簡單與實用，
讓您購物之餘，也能自然而然的學習英文哦。

◆ 相關網頁

➡ **英國女裝以 Topshop 網站為例** （圖片來源: http://www.topshop. com 有 size guide 尺寸導引）

➡ **尺寸表說明**

➢ 如何測量 Measuring：先測量自己的上圍、腰圍和下圍。在尺寸計算器 Size calculator 裡，選擇要查詢的品項，如洋裝、上衣和襯衫，選擇英寸或是公分 inches / cms，輸入測量值，就能算出您的尺寸。

> 尺寸轉換 Conversations：Topshop 為英國網站，尺寸自然為英國尺寸 UK size。Conversation 裡有英國尺寸與其他尺寸對照。
>
> 內衣 Bras：裡面有詳盡的胸圍尺寸，與罩杯尺寸測量方法。
>
> 配件 Accessories：內有領帶，戒指，皮帶及帽子的尺寸測量。
>
> 孕婦 Maternity：大一號的孕婦裝，從 8 號起跳。
>
> 鞋子 Shoes：簡單的尺寸說明。
>
> 品牌 Brands：其他品牌的尺寸表。
>
> 特大號&嬌小 Tall& Petite：特大號&嬌小尺寸的規格。

➡ 美國女裝以 BCBGMAXAZRIA 網站為例

（圖片來源: http://www.bcbg.com）

在商品旁有個尺寸，下方還有試穿鬆緊說明，模特兒資料等。

➡ 童裝以 Oldnavy 網站為例　（圖片來源: http://oldnavy.gap.com）

在商品旁有個尺寸表 Size Chart，點選進去，就可以選擇。

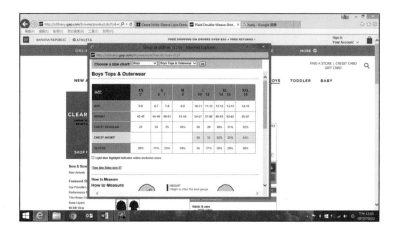

➡ **鞋子以 UGG 網站為例** （圖片來源：http://www.uggaustralia.com/sizing-information.html）

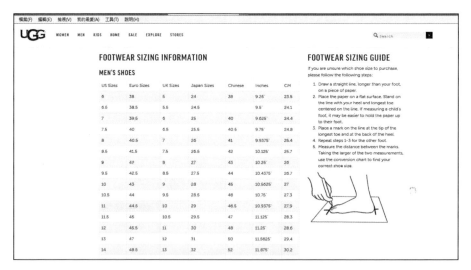

➡ **如何測量（以下為網站尺寸指引譯中）**

Step1：在一張紙上，劃出一條比自己腳長的直線。

Step2：將紙平放，腳踝及最長的腳趾的在紙上。

Step3：在前後 2 端各做記號。

Step4：另一隻腳也重複 1-3 的步驟

Step5：測量您所得到的距離，再到尺寸表找到正確鞋的尺寸。記得鞋的尺寸要比所測量到的 2 腳實際距離稍大。

➡ **尺寸表**

分為

Men's Shoes　　男鞋

Women's Shoes　　女鞋

Kids'Shoes　　童鞋

測量到尺寸之後，再根據男女分類到尺寸表挑選。

 小貼士

➤ 亞洲人的體型通常較歐美人士嬌小，因此在挑選衣物的時候，請一定要先研究尺寸表，不要以台灣習慣的尺碼去購買，若以台灣尺寸去國外網站購買，您收到的尺寸可能會太大。

🎩 **Word Bank**

Size Guide	尺寸指引	Select size	選擇尺寸
Sleeve	袖長	Natural Waist	自然腰圍
Waist	腰圍	High Hip	高臀圍
Low Hip	低臀圍	Inseam	褲檔長
Chest Regular	一般胸圍	Chest Husky	較寬胸圍
Fitted	合身	Stretch	伸縮

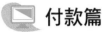 **付款篇**

　　最簡潔的線上購物付款方式即為信用卡，只要輸入相關資料就能輕鬆購物。本篇要告訴您到了結帳網頁時該如何操作。

情境對話

April: I'm starving. Let's order. Meredith, what would you recommend?

我很餓，來點餐吧。Meredith，你推薦什麼好吃的？

Meredith: Well, you can try their steak. It's quite juicy and tender Even my son can have a plate of it. You know how he is. He is so fussy about food.

你要不要試試他們的牛排，滿鮮嫩多汁的。連我兒子都可以吃完一整盤，你也知道他總是對食物很挑的。

April: Ok, then I would like the steak,

好的，那我想點牛排，

Monica?

Monica 你呢？

Monica: I don't have the idea, actually, I kind of lost my appetite.

我不知道，事實上，我有點沒胃口耶。

Meredith: Are you ok? Did you have late breakfast?

你還好嗎？ 是不是早餐吃太晚？

Monica: I virtually ate nothing this morning. It's stomach flu. I had my Dr. checked yesterday. She said the vomiting was the common symptom, and I will recover in few days. But try to avoid the greasy food.

早上沒有吃什麼，是腸胃型感冒。我昨天看過醫生了，她說嘔吐是常見的症狀，應該過幾天就沒事了。但是要避免油膩的食物。

Meredith: Sorry to hear that, why you didn't say anything on the phone? You should stay at home and take some rest.

怎麼會怎樣，電話上怎麼都沒聽你提起？你應該留在家好好休息的。

Monica: Don't worry. I'm better now. No more vomiting. Besides, I don't want to miss this lunch with you . We haven't gotten together for long time.

別擔心，我現在好多了，也沒有再吐了。此外，我不想錯過跟你們的午餐，我們好久沒有聚在一起了。

Part 1 教學篇

Part 2 商品篇

Part 3 旅遊篇

Meredith: Indeed.

的確如此。

Monica: I wish could live nearby. Hey, I really like the gifts from you, can you teach me how to shop on-line? It seems very difficult for me.

希望我能住附近就好。我真的很喜歡你們送我的禮物，可以教我怎麼上網購物嗎？這好像很難。

Meredith: Not at all, first you need a credit card, then fill in some forms. It's quite simple.

一點也不，首先你需要一張信用卡然後填寫一些表格。還滿簡單的哦。

🌐 單字解析

Tender [ˋtɛndɚ] *adj.* 嫩的

例 The steak is overcooked. It is not tender at all.

➜ 那牛排煮太久了，一點都不嫩。

💲 句型解析

本書生活化的對話中為您介紹實用的句型或是短句，再舉例句說明，讓您看完之後，就能馬上輕鬆學會，不用背誦！！

I wish I could 我希望我可以

解 這是一句簡單的假設句，用 can 的過去式 could，來表達與事實相反假設語氣。

I wish I could，我希望我可以，意思是我不能做到某事。

看例句就能理解！！

例 I wish I could go to Denmark this summer, but I have to work.

➡ 我希望我這個夏天能去丹麥，但是我必須工作。

例 I wish I could stay longer, but my car is waiting.

➡ 我希望我能留久一點，但是我的車已經在等我了。

◆ 在個人資料內先建立資料

➡ **在我的帳戶建立信用卡資料 以 UGG 帳號為例**

（圖片來源： https://www.uggaustralia.com）

Payment Settings　　付款設定。

Add Card　　加入信用卡資料。（點選此項，進入填寫）

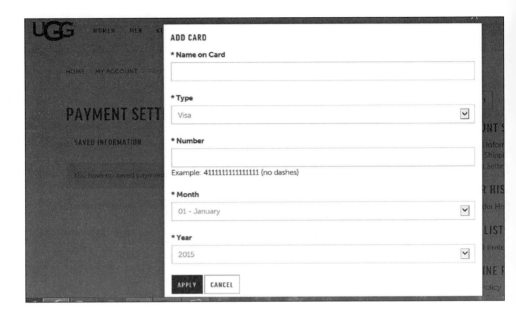

Name on Card　　卡片上的姓名

Type　　卡片種類（通常為 visa 或是 mastercard）

Number　　信用卡卡號（16 碼，不加破折號）

Month　　月份　　Year　　年份

Apply　　提交

在付款網頁填寫

➡ **Payment Details** 付款細節 （圖片來源:http://www.asos.com）

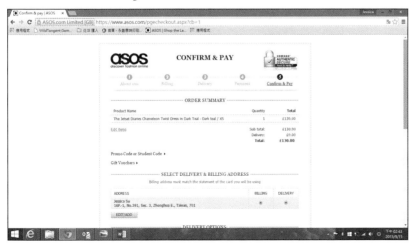

Card Number：填寫卡號

Cardholder Name：持卡人姓名

卡片上有，應與您的護照上中文名字的英文拼音名相同

End Date (mm/yy) 或是 Valid Dates：卡片有效月年

Start Date (mm/yy)：卡片生效月年

➡ Confirm and Pay 確認訂單

信用卡資料輸入完畢之後，會再出現訂單內容以供確認。

這裡還可以輸入促銷碼及選擇送貨地址。

Order Summary　　訂單內容

Promote Code or Student Code　　促銷碼或學生碼

Gift Vouchers　　禮券

➡ Delivery Options 運送選項

➢ 一般來說，免運費的運送時間約為 21 天，這是屬於標準運送 Standard Delivery. 若是您覺得太慢，則可選擇快件寄送 Express，運送時間會縮短至 7 天左右，但是必須支付快件寄送的費用。網站上會讓您自行選擇運送方式。

➢ 都選擇好之後，則會進入最後的付款確認，必須輸入安全碼 Security Code ,也就是您卡片背後 3 位數字。至此，訂單完成，您的信箱也會收到確認信函

Part
1
教學篇

Part
2
商品篇

Part
3
旅遊篇

 信用卡小貼士

➢ 在國外網站消費的支出，雖然我們人在國內，但是仍屬海外消費。因此銀行在每個月結算的時候會另外再跟持卡人收取一筆國外刷卡手續費。一般來說銀行的國外刷卡手續費多為 1.5%.

➢ 另一方面，銀行也針對海外消費需求較高的持卡人，推出了海外刷卡回饋金。如中信卡、台新卡及永豐卡等。聰明的消費者可以在結帳前，先去電信用卡客服中心，了解各卡最優惠的使用方式，再決定要使用哪一張卡來結帳。這樣，又可以省下一筆費用哦。

➢ 有些美國網站，尤其無法提供國際運送的網站，是不接受美國地區以外發行的信用卡。也就是說我們台灣地區發行的信用卡就沒有辦法完成付款。這時候，就可以使用 Paypal 支付。請見 Paypal 篇。

word bank

Payment	付款	Cardholder	持卡人
Billing address	帳單地址	Valid Date	有效期
Delivery address	運送地址		

💻 第三方支付 **Paypal** 篇

　　線上購物網站十分便捷，選擇也多。購物之後，我們會在許多不同的網站留下信用卡資料。雖說許多購物網站都對於交易安全十分重視，其實還有另一個選擇 Paypal.

💎 情境對話

Meredith: April, Keith just called. They would like to revise the mold drawing. Can you get it done before this Friday?

April，Keith 剛打電話來，他們想要更改模具的設計圖，你有辦法在這週五之前完成嗎？

April: Which mold? We have 4 different molds in Design Department.

哪一個模具，設計部門有四個不同的模具。

Meredith: It's the rim #2251. For the wheelbarrow.

編號#2251，獨輪車用的鋼圈。

April: No problem. I can finish it before this Friday. Actually, since I already finished my work this morning, I can start this assignment right away. What would you say?

沒問題，這週五可以完成。其實，今天早上我所有的工作都已經完成了，我馬上就可以開始做這項任務，你覺得如何？

Meredith: Even better! I really appreciate it. You know how valuable this client is. Keith's order is significant for the company. We have to handle his request carefully and promptly.

再好也不過了！真的很謝謝你。你知道我們很重視 Keith 這位客戶，他的訂單對公司十分重要。對於他的要求我們必須迅速地謹慎處理。

April: Totally agree with you. I'm right on it. Before that, may I ask you something?

完全同意你。我馬上去做，在這之前，可以先問一件事嗎？

Meredith: Sure.

當然。

April: For the internet shopping, I had changed my credit card billing address to mailing address. But, why do some websites are still reluctant to accept my credit card?

為了網路購物，我將我的帳單地址修改與我的寄送地址一致。但是，有些網站還是拒絕接受我的信用卡，這是為什麼呢？

Meredith: Probably because your billing address is in not in The States. Did you read their payment term?

有可能是因為你的帳單地址不在美國境內，你有讀網上的付款條件嗎？

April: No, should I ?

沒有，需要嗎？

Meredith: Definitely, you are working in a international trade company. You should know better. Payment term is always critical. Show me the website.

一定需要的。妳自己在國際貿易公司上班，你應該比誰都清楚，付款條件總是最重要的，讓我看看那個網站。

單字解析

Request [rɪ`kwɛst] *v./n.* 要求

例 No one can reject his request. He is an adorable kid.

➜ 他是討人喜歡的小孩，沒有人能拒絕得了他的要求。

句型解析

本書生活化的對話中為您介紹實用的句型或是短句，再舉例句說明，讓您看完之後，就能馬上輕鬆學會，不用背誦！！

I'm right on it 我馬上去辦

解 通常在公司裡，上司對下屬交代事項，下屬聽到之後表示我們認同對

方所說的話，並且會馬上去處理，就能這樣說。十分口語的一句話，
沒有困難的單字，您一定能學會。

例 A: Monica, I need the financial report of last season.
　　B: No problem. I'm right on it.

→ A: Monica，我需要上的月的財務報告。
　　B: 沒問題，我馬上去辦！

以上的單字及短句十分的簡單與實用，
讓您購物之餘，也能自然而然的學習英文哦。

💎 相關網站 - **Paypal** 申請流程

→ **Paypal** 註冊　（畫面來源 https://www.paypal.com/tw/webapps/mpp/home）

目前 Paypal 已有中文界面，只需一步步驟填寫資料。

完成註冊之後會看到我的帳戶。而您註冊的信箱也會收到來自 Paypal 的確認信。確認之後，**請您在帳戶中新增信用卡。**

➡ 新增信用卡於我的帳戶

這張信用卡就是以後在 Paypal 中付款的帳戶。

因為要跟發卡銀行做確認，所以最後由發卡銀行郵寄一封密碼函給

您，這個確認的動作花費 NT70，由銀行收取。之後 Paypal 會在您的
Paypal 帳戶裡扣除。

一般用戶在 Paypal 註冊之後，輸入相關資料，確認好細節之後，
會得到一組 Paypal 帳號。

從此用此帳號，就可在有 Paypal 的網家購物，無需再次輸入信用
卡資料。

💎 為什麼需要使用 Payal

您或許認為有信用卡不論是 Viva 或是 Mastercard 都是國際機構發行的國際信用卡。但是因為網路安全的關係，防止盜刷，**有些網路商家，以美國為例，不接受美國地區以外發行的信用卡**，或是帳單地址不在美國境內的信用卡。您會看到網站說明如下：

If you are using an international credit card (Visa, MasterCard, American Express, Discover) that utilizes a billing address within the United States, we would be able to place an order and ship to an address within the United States or the U.S. Territories. We are unable to support the use of international billing addresses.

中譯：如果您所使用的國際信用卡（Visa,MasterCard,American Express,Discover）是登記在美國境內的地址。我們樂於接單並運送到美國境內的地址。 我們無法接受在帳單地址在美國境外的國際信用卡。

遇到這種情形，您可選擇使用 Palpay 付款，再由轉運公司代運送回台灣（請見轉運公司篇）。

Paypal 小貼士

➢ Paypal 是否需要支付手續費?

　　Paypal 的使用戶在申請時就區分為網路購物使用戶,收款專用的商業用戶。而我們就屬**網路購物使用戶**,而非賣家,針對網路購物一般來說是不需手續費用的,但是若是跨國購物,可能有貨幣轉換的費用。而銀行會在我們收取 Paypal 款項時,會再跟我們加收國外交易費用,因為 Paypal 為國外公司哦。

　　以上網站的資訊僅為參考,實際規則以您實際購物時,網站所公布規則為準。

Word Bank

International	國際的	Credit Card	信用卡
Address	地址	Territories	領土
Billing Addresses	帳單地址		

Part 1 教學篇

Part 2 商品篇

Part 3 旅遊篇

運費篇

國際購物讓人最在意的除了商品之外，就是運費成本了。本篇要告訴如何看懂網站上的運費規定，找到國際運送的條款，了解相關運費。

情境對話

April: Here it is. The drawing of rim #2251. I had altered it according to Keith's request. The specification of rim outer is smaller.

鋼圈#2251 的設計圖在這裡，依照 Keith 的要求做了修改，鋼圈的外圈規格比較小了。

Meredith: Let me check it again. Well done!! I'm very impressed by your work efficiency , April.

讓我再確認一次，做得好！！你的工作效率讓我很驚訝，April。

April: Not a problem. I am quite proficient in Solidwork. Honestly speak-

這很簡單的，我對 Solidwork 這套軟體很

ing, I prefer software work to sales work. I always can concentrate my mind on drawing. It makes me peaceful.

熟。老實説，我對軟體工作比業務工作有興趣多。當繪圖的時候，我總是很專注，繪圖能為我帶來平靜。

Meredith: Then, you will be our drawing specialist in the sales department .. We really need it.

那麼，你以後就是銷售部門的繪圖專家。我們真的很需要。

April: Thanks, look forward to starting the assignment.

謝謝，對我的新工作期待不已。

Meredith: So, did you get the Coach bag online?

那麼，你有買到那個 Coach 包嗎？

April: It's a long story. Well, at the beginning, I found that price difference was not much. Besides, I had to pay for the shipping cost and custom tax. After calculating all the cost over and over again, I decided not to buy it.

説來話長。一開始的時候，價差不大。而且我還必須支付運費跟關税費用等。我再三計算過所有的成本之後，我覺得還是算了。

Meredith: Well, you are smart. You

那你很聰明，知道下單前

look at all the cost before placing the order.

要先把所有的費用先查清楚。

April: Ha, I learn from the best. But after 2 week, it's on sale and it's 70% off. Can you believe that? How can I miss it? The price difference is huge, so I placed the order last night.

哈，名師出高徒嘛～。但是 2 周之後，網站開始特價，而且折扣 70%，你能相信嗎？我怎麼能錯過呢？這樣一來，價差變得好大，所以昨天晚上，我就下單了。

🌐 單字解析

Concentrate [`kɑnsɛnˌtret] *v./n.* 專心

例 Can you please quite? I try to concentrate on my work

➜ 能請你安靜嗎？我試著要專心工作。

📋 句型解析

 本書生活化的對話中為您介紹實用的句型或是短句，再舉例句說明，讓您看完之後，就能馬上輕鬆學會，不用背誦！！

Someone + be impressed by Something
某人對某是感到印象深刻

解 這裡的印象深刻，指的是好的印象。其中 impress 表示為欽佩，印象良好之意。

例 We were impressed by Copenhagen, it's a friendly city.

➡ 我們對哥本哈根印象深刻，那真是個友善的城市。

例 The teacher was impressed by Owen's talent, he plays Go very well.

➡ 老師對 Owen 的天分印象深刻，他的圍棋下得很好。

以上的單字及短句十分的簡單與實用，
讓您購物之餘，也能自然而然的學習英文哦。

💎 相關網站 1

➡ **運費列在 Help**（圖片來源網址：http://www.uggaustralia.com/）

Step1 看運費:請在首頁先將網頁拉到最下方。找到 Help（幫助）
中的 Shipping（運送）。點進去。點選進去之後，通常網
站會就其所在地做詳細的運費說明，如美國地區，標準運
送，快遞運送的費用跟天數等。而我們要採國際運送往下
拉，會看到這個字 International shipping

Step2 找到國際運送 International shipping

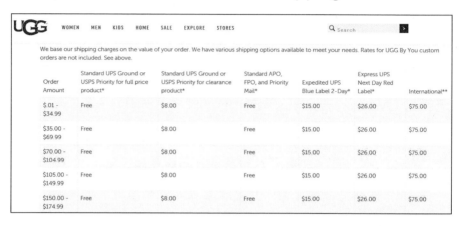

We base our shipping charges on the value of your order. We have various shipping options available to meet your needs. Rates for UGG By You custom orders are not included. See above.

Order Amount	Standard UPS Ground or USPS Priority for full price product*	Standard UPS Ground or USPS Priority for clearance product*	Standard APO, FPO, and Priority Mail*	Expedited UPS Blue Label 2-Day*	Express UPS Next Day Red Label*	International**
$.01 - $34.99	Free	$8.00	Free	$15.00	$26.00	$75.00
$35.00 - $69.99	Free	$8.00	Free	$15.00	$26.00	$75.00
$70.00 - $104.99	Free	$8.00	Free	$15.00	$26.00	$75.00
$105.00 - $149.99	Free	$8.00	Free	$15.00	$26.00	$75.00
$150.00 - $174.99	Free	$8.00	Free	$15.00	$26.00	$75.00

　　以 UGG 網站為例，運費做成表格十分清楚。您可看到運費是根據訂單金額計算，而國際運送不論金額多少，運費一律 USD$75。

💎 相關網站 2

➡ **首頁就看得到運費**（圖片來源網址： http://www.topshop.com/）

Step1 看運費:現在的網站有的會自動偵測 IP，我們連上時，就已知道是台灣的顧客。所以您在畫面左上角會看到台灣國旗，並有寫 Free shipping find out more.（免運費，按此查看）

Step2 點選進去:國際運送 International delivery 國際運送，選擇國家 Taiwan . 運費就會顯示。

➡ 所有 £100 以上的訂單，標準運送免費。若想知道你寄送國家標準運送及快遞運送詳情，請下拉選單。

台灣：標準運送 8 個工作天，運費 £10.5。

　　　快遞運送 3 個工作天，運費 £20.0。

相關網站 3

➡ **完全不提供國際運送** （圖片來源：https://help.sanuk.com）

首頁下方的 help 中找到 shipping information 運送資訊中，説明完全不提供送國際運送。

💎 相關網站 4

➡ 有國際運送，但是台灣不在運送範圍

（圖片來源網址：https://www.katespade.com）

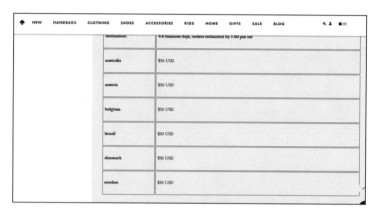

在 Kate Spade 網站的運送方式與運費 Shipping methods and Costs 裡的國際運費 international rates 中，列出了寄送的國家。但是沒有台灣，表示台灣不在運送範圍之內。

❤ 小貼士

➢ 舉例來説，一只包手袋在台灣專櫃售價 20,000，而國外網站折扣下來只有 10,000，十分讓人心動。但是在下手之前，請先研究運費、關税及信用卡的手續費等。全部都加總才是這項商品上我們所需付出的成本，而非網站的商品價格 10,000 而已。當您都算出來之後，發現商品加上其他費用價格仍十分有優勢，如此，才是下手的時機。

> 但若是追求時尚的消費者，最新、最流行的商品才能符合需求，這時運費或關稅就不是考慮的重點。消費者可以針對自己的消費模式到適合的商家購物。

> 以上網站的運費資訊僅為參考，各個網站有時會出免運費活動，或是更改運送規則。實際運費以您實際購物時，網站所公布的規則為準。

Word Bank

Customer Service	顧客服務	Shipping	運送
Shipping rates	運送費用	International Shipping	國際運送
International Delivery	國際運送	Standard delivery	標準運送
Express delivery	快遞運送	Free shipping	免費運送

Part 1 教學篇

Part 2 商品篇

Part 3 旅遊篇

網站不寄送
試試轉運

◆ 轉運是什麼

　　許多美國的網站，美國境內享有低門檻的運費，但沒有運送國外。這時候還有另一個選擇，轉運公司。轉運公司會提供一個美國地址給您，收網路的貨物，再由轉運公司安排運送回台灣。

◆ 情境對話

April: Meredith, Christian and I are going to the bar. Want to join us?

Meredith，Christian 跟我要去酒吧，你要一起去嗎？

Meredith: Sure! It's Friday night. I don't want to stay in my apartment alone with TV. It's miserable. Which bar ?

當然，我可不想在星期五晚上一個人待在家裡看電視，那真是可悲。你們要去哪個酒吧？

April: Smoky Jo. Hey, I want to buy

冒煙的 Jo。嘿，我想在

a bag online, but it says that the international shipping is not available. What am I supposed to do?

網路上買個手提袋。但是網站說不提供國際運送，那我該怎麼辦？

Meredith: Well, there are a bunch of companies who offer buying & shipping service. You can tell them which item you are interested in, then they will buy it for you and ship it to your Taiwan address. Besides the freight, there are some handling fees for sure.

網路上有許多代購或是代運的服務。你跟他們聯絡之後告訴他們你想買什麼，然後代購公司會幫你買好，寄到你台灣的家裡。當然，除了運費之外，還需要支付手續費雜費等。

April: That sounds very convenient, but I <u>prefer to</u> keep the shopping pleasure for myself. How about the shipping service?

聽起來很方便，但是我這樣我就無法享受購物的樂趣了。那代運公司服務項目為何？

Meredith: First, you should register on the website, then they will provide a valid American address to you.

首先，你必須在網路上先註冊。然後他們會給你一組有效的美國境內地址。

April: With the real America address, I can continue shopping.

有了這個美國地址，我就可以繼續購物了。

Meredith: Yes, but before that, re-

沒錯，但是你得要先了解

Part
1
教學篇

Part
2
商品篇

Part
3
旅遊篇

member to read the payment term, make sure that international credit card is acceptable.

付款條件，確定能使用國際信用卡。

April: Don't worry, if it's not acceptable. I got paypal. I have already applied a paypal account.

別擔心，如果不可以的話，我還有 Paypal，我已經申請好 Paypal 的帳號了。

Meredith: <u>You do have</u> a persistent passion on shopping.

你對購物真是有熱情呀

單字解析

Apply [ə`plaɪ] *v.* 申請

例 James had applied for the field trip in November.

➔ James 申請了 11 月的戶外教學

句型解析

 本書生活化的對話中為您介紹實用的句型或是短句，再舉例句說明，讓您看完之後，就能馬上輕鬆學會，不用背誦!!

S+ prefer to 我比較喜歡…／我寧願…

解 1: prefer 喜愛。通常 prefer 是二種事物比較之後，有一個是比較喜歡的。喜歡的要放在 prefer 後面。

例 I prefer shopping to working.

➡ 我喜歡逛物勝於工作。

解 2: 有時候，並不會將 2 件事一併列入，而是前面句子已經提到了，
我們再說 I prefer……

例 The weather is so hot. I prefer to stay at home.

➡ 天氣很熱，我寧願待在家裡。

以上的單字及短句十分的簡單與實用，
讓您購物之餘，也能自然而然的學習英文哦。

💎 相關網站

➡ **代運流程**（舉例網站說明: comGateway 代運公司）

（圖片來源網址：https://secure.comgateway.com/）

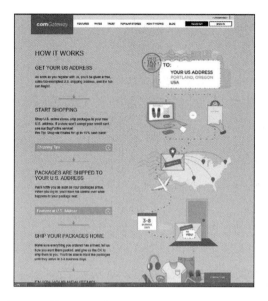

➡ 首頁有清楚的說明代運的流程

Step1. 註冊之後，可以得到一個免費的美國地址。若原購物網站不接受我們的台灣信用卡，可請這代運公司代購

Step2. 等商品寄到您的美國地址之後，會收到通知。當您登入代運公司網站之後，就能決定是否要安排運送，還是等其他商品到齊一起運送。

Step3. 決定運送時，通知代運公司。

➡ 關於代運的費用

⇒ **comgateway** 運費表說明

快遞運送：首重 0.5 公斤起價美元$13.57，美元$3.74／每續重半
公斤。

標準運送：首重 0.5 公斤起價美元$11.80，美元$3.25／每續重半
公斤。

⇒ **comgateway** 其他費用：分有一般會員與白金會員。

一般會員：運費如上，沒有折扣。

代購費 5%。

集合包裝費：首三件免費，之後每單件收美元$1.0／件

重新包裝費：箱子改小，美元$7.0，裝箱改成袋裝美元
$5.0

倉儲費用：30 天內免費，超過 30 天美元$1.0／天

◆ 其他代運網站

⇒ **MyUS.com**（圖片來源網址：https://www.myus.com/）

（網站說明：美國的代運公司，可以先輸入國家，包裹重量估算運費。）

Part
1
教學篇

Part
2
商品篇

Part
3
旅遊篇

➡ **GlobalShopex.com** （圖片來源網址: http://www.globalshopex. com）（網站說明:美國的代運公司。）

小貼士

➢ 在 comGateway 網站中，有個 weight guide 重量參考，會告訴您 一雙鞋，一個包包大概重量多少。如此您便可試算運費。

➤ 基於國際網物的興起，也有台灣的公司在做代運或是代運/代購的服務。這些公司都是中文介面，本篇就不多做說明。想要參考的話，請使用網路搜尋"美國代運" "這類關鍵字就能找到。

➤ 這類服務性質的網站，選擇多。除了運費價格之外，也必須將服務的完整性和客服人員反應的即時性一併納入考慮。才能找到適合您的代運公司。

➤ 以上網站的運費資訊僅為參考，各個網站有時更改運送規則。實際運費以您實際購物時，網站所公布的規則為準。

Word Bank

Prime	高級	Package	包裹
Arrive	到達	Estimate	預估
Rate Table	費用表	Repack	重新包裝
Storage	倉儲	Weights Guilds	重量參考
Shipping Cost	運送成本	Speed of Delivery	運送速度
Combining of Package	集合包裹		

Part 1 教學篇

Part 2 商品篇

Part 3 旅遊篇

關稅篇

　　本篇要告訴您政府課稅的標準是什麼，常買的衣服、鞋、包等稅率是要怎麼試算。簡單搞懂關稅，網路購物一樣輕鬆！！

情境對話

April: Meredith, I just received phone call from DHL about my parcel. They told me that I have to pay NT600 tariff to release it. I didn't know that there is such a regulation. Is this a blackmail or bluff?

Meredith，我剛接到 DHL 的電話說我買的包裹有問題。説我必須付 600 元的關稅才能放行。我沒聽過這項規定，會不會是詐欺，還是在騙我？

Meredith: I don't think so. How much of your order?

應該不會，你的訂單金額是多少呢？

Part
1
教學篇

Part
2
商品篇

Part
3
旅遊篇

April: Around NT15,000. I got a leather jacket and several dresses. It's on sale, with 25% additional discount. <u>Can't miss it</u>

差不多台幣 15,000,我買了件皮夾克跟幾件洋裝。因為有特價，可以多折扣 25％，不想錯過呢。

Meredith: Well, if the order value is over NT3,000, according to the custom regulation, you <u>are supposed to</u> pay for the tariff.

如果訂單金額超過台幣 3000 元根據海關法就要付關稅哦。

April: Are you sure? My last order was NT6,000, and there was no such tariff notice.

真的嗎？可是我上次買了 6000 元也沒這個問題呀？

Meredith: You were just lucky. I had paid the tariff many times.

你上次比較幸運。我付過很多次關稅了呢。

April: Ok, as long as it's not blackmail, I'm glad to pay for the tariff. Well, it's good citizen's obligation. Right? Besides, even with the tariff, it's still worthy.

好吧，只要不是詐騙就好了。付關稅沒有關係，本來就是國民的義務，是吧？而且，即使加上關稅還是很划算的。

Meredith: You are absolutely right.

說的一點都沒錯，你知道

Hey, you know you can check the tariff rate in advance on customs website. I usually do that before placing the order. It's very convenient and easy to understand.

嗎？ 其實你可以事先在海關網站上查出稅率。通常我在下訂單前會先查清楚關稅，很方便使用也簡單易懂。

April: Wow! You are the expert!! Show me the website.

哇！你真的是專家，給我看海關網站吧。

🌐 單字解析

Tariff [`tærɪf] *n./v.* 關稅

例 The tariff of luxury car in Taiwan is very high.

➜ 台灣高級房車的關稅很高。

💲 句型解析

本書生活化的對話中為您介紹實用的句型或是短句，再舉例句說明，讓您看完之後，就能馬上輕鬆學會，不用背誦!!

S+ be supposed to 按規定應當的

解 當我們要說明一件事情或是本應該如何時，我們可以用 supposed to

例 Lisa is supposed to show up today. She made the appointment last month.

➔ Lisa 今天應該要來的，她上個月就預訂好了。

例 I was supposed to finish those work before Friday.

➔ 我本應該在星期五前完成這些工作的。

Can't miss it 不能錯過

解 這裡的 miss 不當想念，而是當錯過之意。

例 Hurry up, the training is coming . I don't want to miss it.

➔ 快點，火車來了，我不想錯過它。

以上的單字及短句十分的簡單與實用，

讓您購物之餘，也能自然而然的學習英文哦。

◆ 相關網頁介紹

➔ **關稅規定 財政部網站 http://www.etax.nat.gov.tw 如下**

（稅率查詢 http://portal.sw.nat.gov.tw/）

➡ **輸入要查詢的產品如：鞋**

會出現該產品的稅率

有第一欄、第二欄、第三欄不同的稅率。

第一欄為 WTO 會員國的稅率，通常我們網購的國家多在此欄。

第二欄則是特別簽訂免稅條款的國家。

　　以鞋來説，若是價值超過台幣 3000 元，被海關驗貨抽到的稅率則為 5%。除了進口關稅之外，尚有營業稅 5%（這是固定的），即使我們在網上購買的商品是自用而非營業買賣用，還是必須付此項費用哦。

若是對進口關稅有任何問題，除了上財政部網站查詢之外，亦可直接打電話到財政部詢問。

稅則號別分類、稅率疑義及服務專線

TEL: (02) 25505500 轉#1020

➡ **各網站規定**

除了海關網站可查詢之外，購物平台網站，針對此項費用各有不同做法，說明如下

➡ **1. 不包含關稅等費用**

➢ Taxes and Duties

We ship your package DDU, "duties and taxes unpaid", and we do not collect nor do we calculate the VAT, duties and/or taxes during checkout.

Any fees that are due will be collected upon delivery of the order. For more information regarding your country's custom policies, please contact your local customs office.

➔ 關稅說明

我們所寄送的包裹是不包含關稅及貨物稅的。所有的相關費用會在貨物**抵達時支付**。需要更多資訊請向當地政府海關單位查詢。

解 表示該網站結帳的金額，僅是商品金額。商品進到台灣海關時，可能會被抽驗到支付關稅等。若想事先知道此項費用，可在購物時先上稅率查詢網站。 http://portal.sw.nat.gov.tw/

Part 1 教學篇

Part 2 商品篇

Part 3 旅遊篇

⇒ **2. 商品結帳包含關稅等費用**

➢ Taxes and Duties

At checkout we guarantee a landed cost shipping for all international purchases which includes shipping, duties, taxes, tariffs, etc. and we will also handle all of the brokerage fees.

➔ 結帳時我們保證所有的費用包含:國際運費，貨物稅，關稅，清關費用等都已內含。

You can now shop our site and see your complete order total, including shipping and importation fees (estimated costs for customs, tariffs, and tax) when you check out. Once you submit your order, the total is guaranteed and you will not be charged any additional fees at delivery.

➔ 在我們網站上購物，當您提交訂單時，您的訂單金額，包含運送費用、進口費用（預估的關稅，貨物稅）都會包含在內。貨物送達時您無需支付任何其他費用。

🈟 上面 2 則都是說明，在結帳時，除了商品的金額之外，運費跟關稅等進口費用，都會一併結算。我們必須先支付這筆費用，易言之，當商品到目的地時，會直接送達，我們就不用支付其他費用。

❤ 關稅小貼士

➢ 在國外許多明明是平價、價格可親的品牌，到我們的百貨商家上架之後卻變得高不可攀。這時候精打細算的您就可以利用網路購物挑選喜歡的商品。

➤ 雖説要支付關稅，但是只要我們事先做好工作，查詢清楚，就能開開心心地購物。不但能擁有最新的流行商品，而且您會發現大多數的商品即使加上關稅等費用還是很划算的。

 # Word Bank

DDU (Delivery Duty Unpaid) 目的地關稅未付		Collect　收取	
Delivery Destination	運送目的地	Charge	索費
Delivery	運送	Duties	稅
Taxes	稅	Vat	營業稅
Tariffs	關稅	Custom	海關

如何退貨

在國外網站購物時，若是收到的商品有瑕疵時該怎麼辦呢？ 請先跟網站的客服人員聯繫吧。本篇要告訴您遇到這類狀況時，如何填寫退貨單，及該如何以英文書信跟國外客服人員溝通。

情境對話

Meredith: April, did you get the parcel from DHL？

April，你收到 DHL 的包裹了嗎？

April: Yep, I received my parcel yesterday. The dresses are very elegant for formal occasion. You know, I have to attend my sister's wedding next Friday. But the leather jacket is such a disaster. There are some grey mold on it.

有的，昨天拿到的。洋裝很優雅適合正式場合穿，你知道我下週要參加我妹妹的婚禮。但是皮衣就很糟糕，上面居然有灰色的黴斑。

Meredith: Are you kidding me?Oh! It's so gross.

不會吧，天呀！好噁心。

April: Tell me about it . Now I don't know what to do with that jacket. Do you think dry clean can remove the mold?

還用得著你説嗎，現在我正為此傷腦筋。你覺得送乾洗能去除黴班嗎？

Meredith: I'm not sure. Are you keeping the jacket? Why don't you return it?

這我不清楚，但是你要留著這件皮衣嗎？為什麼不退貨呢？

April: Can I do that? I don't know how to talk about this with foreigners.

可以這麼做嗎？我不知道怎麼跟外國人談這事呀。

Meredith: Don't worry, first you can email the company, inform them that you received a poor quality jacket and give them your order no. They will reply you.

別擔心，首先你先寫封電子郵件給網路公司告知他們收到一件瑕疵的皮衣，並附上你的訂單號碼，然後他們就會回覆你的。

April: But who is going to pay for the return freight and can I get my tariff back ?

那退貨的運費由誰支付呢？ 我之前付的關稅能拿回來嗎？

Part

1

教學篇

Part

2

商品篇

Part

3

旅遊篇

Meredith: It depends. Each company has a different return policy. That's why we should send an e-mail to them first. Do you keep the proof of tariff?

那不一定，因為每家公司的退貨規定不盡相同。這就是為什麼我們要先寫信給客服人員。你的完稅證明還有留著嗎？

April: Yes, it's on the top of parcel.

有，就黏在包裹上面。

Meredith: Good, you may need it.

好，可能妳會需要它。

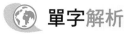 **單字**解析

Formal KK[`fɔrm!] *adj.* 正式的

例 The formal application is valid, so he got the job.

➔ 正式的申請是有效的，所以他得到了新的工作。

句型解析

 本書生活化的對話中為您介紹實用的句型或是短句，再舉例句說明，讓您看完之後，就能馬上輕鬆學會，不用背誦！！

Tell me about it 用得著你說嗎？

解 光看句子的中文意思是再多說一點，其實真正的涵義是，用得著你說嗎？意思是我認同你的論點，而且這件事我早就如此覺得。

例 A: Our neighbor's dog kept barking last night. It's annoying.

B: Tell me about it. I hardly slept last night.

➜ A: 我們鄰居的狗昨天晚上叫個不停，很煩人。

B: 還用到著你說嗎？　我昨晚幾乎沒睡。

以上的單字及短句十分的簡單與實用，
讓您購物之餘，也能自然而然的學習英文哦。

關於退貨

➜ **Return policy** 退貨條款

　　購物網站上都會有 return policy 退貨條款。針對不同地區（當地客戶、國際客戶）適用不同的退貨條款。當地客戶能享有在規定日期內不喜歡就能有免運費退貨。而**國際客戶**的退貨規定則不太一樣。有的網站是免運費退貨，有的是需要消費者自行支付退貨運費。建議您先看清楚各家的退貨條款。

　　以 A 網站的退貨條款說明

Returns and exchanges for international orders

You can return an item received in an international order, but exchanges are not possible at this time. Instead, you can return the unwanted item and order a new replacement separately. The customer is responsible for the return shipping cost.

➜ 你所收到的國際訂單商品，可以退回，但是不接受換貨。退回不想要的商品之後，請重新下單。退貨費用由消費者支付

解 幾乎所有的網站都是這樣規定，僅退貨，不換貨，客戶支付退貨費用。

Refunds include duties, taxes, and tariffs. Unfortunately, we cannot refund your original international shipping charges.

➜ 退款包含：關稅、營業稅等。但是，原本您支付的運費無法退還。

解 這家網站，會退還客戶支付的關稅等，屬於比較少見的狀況。所以收到國際包裹時，請先確保所有單據的完整性，如此，要退費才有所依據。

以 B 網站的退貨條款說明

International Returns

You must return your items to the address below within 30 days from the day you received your package. Please write your order # on the outside of the package. You will receive your refund in the original form of payment. Unfortunately, we cannot refund duties, taxes, or shipping charges. The customer is responsible for the return shipping cost.

➜ 退貨必須在商品收到的 30 天內，請在退貨包裹上寫上訂單號碼。退貨金額將會退回至您原來付款的帳戶。很抱歉，我們無法退還關稅等費用，以及運費。退貨費用由消費者支付。

解 大部分的網站退貨規定是如此的，消費者不喜歡的商品，可以退回，但是關稅及運費是無法退回的。然而，若是商家寄錯商品，或是商品

收到已有瑕疵等，商家出錯而消費者已支付相關費用時，這時候，就建議您可以寫信給客戶服務人員，爭取關稅等費用。

Refunds and Processing

Refunds will be processed within approximately 7 to 10 business days after we receive your return.

Original shipping charges are non-refundable.

➡ 在我們收到您的退貨包裹後的 7-10 個工作日安排退款，原運費不退回。

➡ **Returns note** 退貨單

一般寄達的包裹中，都會有 returns note 退貨單。收件人可視情況填寫，常見的退貨單上都會有退貨原因。這裡舉例說明

· Looks different to image on site	貨品跟網頁上看起來不一樣
· Ordered more than one size	尺寸太大
· Arrived too late	太晚到貨
· Poor Quality/faulty	品質不佳
· Doesn't fit properly	不合身
· Doesn't suit me	不適合我
· Incorrect item received	產品送錯
· Parcel damaged on arrival	包裹送達時已破損

➡ 關於退貨書信往來

遇到要退貨的情況，建議您要退貨之前，先去信給網站客服人員，說

Part 1 教學篇

Part 2 商品篇

Part 3 旅遊篇

明退貨原因，了解退貨的運費由哪一方支付。

可參考以下書信

Dear Sir

I received my order no.6602. However, it's not the item I purchased

My order is

Item: Woman shoes #2016, size 36

Color: black

In Your Parcel

Item: Woman shoes #2016, size 36

Color: Red

Return reason: Incorrect item received

Therefore, I would like to return this parcel. Please advise how to do it

您好

我收到訂單號 6602，但是這非我購買的產品

我的訂單是

項目：女鞋 #2016，尺碼 36

顏色：黑色

在收到的包裹為

項目：女鞋 #2016，尺碼 36

顏色：紅色

退貨原因：產品送錯

因此我要辦理退貨，請告訴我該如何處理。

學會了嗎？可以在退貨理由上換加入您實際的狀況，就能跟國外商家溝通。

退貨小貼士

➤ 若準備退貨，填寫好 Returns note 退貨單。並請保持商品完整性，保留原有的吊牌及包裝。因為商家在收到退貨商品時，必須檢查商品是否完整。商品若有損傷或是商家覺得已經有使用過的跡象，退貨很有可能被拒哦。

➤ 退貨包裹上必須以英文註明為 "Returned Goods" 退貨。這樣才能避免關稅問題哦。

➤ 一般國際退貨約需 14-21 天處理，是包裹寄達的速度。商家收到包裹檢查無誤之後，如無爭議就會安排退款

Part
1
教學篇

Part
2
商品篇

Part
3
旅遊篇

📺 亞馬遜

　　本篇要介紹強大的亞馬遜，如果印象還停留在亞馬遜只是書店的話，會錯過許多好東西的。一起來看看亞馬遜還有賣什麼。

💎 情境對話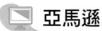

Meredith: Christina, here is the monthly report, please forward it to general manager. And make appointment with Mr. Taylor this afternoon, I would like to meet him at 3 PM.

Christina，這是月報告，麻煩轉給總經理。幫我跟 Mr. Taylor 約好下午 3 點開會，我有點事要跟他討論。

Christina: OK, the rim specification will be ready before that.

好的，我會在這之前將鋼圈的規格表準備好。

Meredith: I hope that we can come

希望今天能有個最後結

to a conclusion today, the rim specification has been pending for a
week. It's not a good sign, we are
unable to solve the problem.

Christina: I believe that Mr. Taylor
will be convinced by our research
report. The rim specification has to
be revised.

Meredith: I have to be very persuasive this afternoon.

Christina: Don't worry, I have faith
in you. Hey, I like your jacket. It looks
so warm. Where did you get it ?

Meredith: Amazon.

Christina: Amazon? That's a bookstore. You must be kidding.

Meredith: No, I'm not. Amazon is not
only a bookstore but also one of the

果，鋼圈規格的問題懸而
未決已經一個星期了。這
不是件好事，我們沒有解
決問題的能力。

相信我們的研究報告能夠
說服 Mr. Taylor 鋼圈規
格必須要修正。

下午我得要表現得說服力
十足。

別擔心，我對你有信心。
嘿，我喜歡你的外套，看
起來很保暖，你哪裡買
的？

亞馬遜

亞馬遜？那不是書店嗎？
你開玩笑的吧！

沒有哦，亞馬遜不光是書
店，他還是線上最大的購

biggest online shopping website. There are thousands shops on Amazon.

物網站之一。亞馬遜上有上千家商家。

Christina: Wow, I'm surprised to hear that.

哇，真是讓人驚訝。

Meredith: Last year, we had family trip to Hokkaido, Japan. It was so cold, the temperature was only-15. My Columbia jacket still kept me warm. So, I bought another Columbia jacket this year on amazon.com, because they offer international shipping.

去年，我們去日本北海道家族旅遊，天氣好冷，氣溫才零下 15 度。靠著 Columbia 外套，我還是覺得很溫暖。所以我今年又在亞馬遜上買 Columbia 外套，因為他們有國際運送。

 單字解析

Specification [ˌspɛsəfəˈkeʃən] *n.* 規格

例 The specification of radial tire needs to be updated.

➜ 那個子午線輪胎的規格必須更新。

句型解析

本書生活化的對話中為您介紹實用的句型或是短句，再舉例句說明，讓您看完之後，就能馬上輕鬆學會，不用背誦！！

1. have faith in Someone　對某人有信心

解 簡單的一句話就可以激勵人心。

例 We have faith in you, you can finish the treatment course. Don't give up.

➔ 我們對你有信心，你可以完成治療的課程的，不要放棄。

2. Not only ...but also ...　不但…還…

解 這是一個很基本句型，用來表示 2 種並存的現象。

例 Patricia is not only a dancer but also a musician .

➔ Patricia 不但是位舞者也是位音樂家。

例 We not only cleaned the house but also washed the car.

➔ 我們不但整理了房子，也洗了車。

以上的單字及短句十分的簡單與實用，
讓您購物之餘，也能自然而然的學習英文哦。

💎 相關網站

➔ **Amazon** （圖片來源：網址 http://www.amazon.com）

Part 1 教學篇

Part 2 商品篇

Part 3 旅遊篇

網頁介紹：美國最大的電商之一，其商品十分多樣化。

國際運送：有寄送台灣，結帳時會連同關稅的費用一併計算。

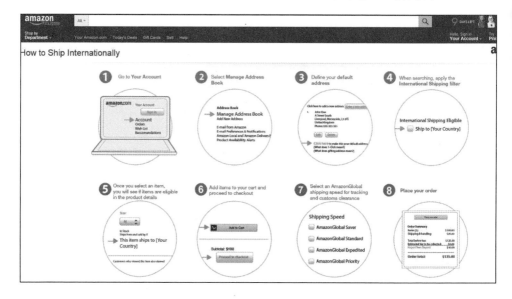

➡ 如何安排國際運送

Step1. Go to your account　　登入帳號

Step2. Manage Address book　　管理地址

Step3. Define your default address　　確認默認地址

Step4. When searching, apply the international shipping filter

搜索時，選擇國際運送選項。

Step5. 當搜索某項商品時，就能知道是否能寄送自己國家。

Step6. 將該項可運送到自己國家的商品，加入購物車，結帳。

Step7. 選擇亞馬遜國際運送選項。

Step8. 下單（您可以看到商品費用、運費、稅，及進口稅都已列出）

（圖片來源：網址 http://www.amazon.com）

左上角有個 Shop by department 依部門購物，選到女裝部門

➡ 1. 網頁介紹：有各式品牌女裝

➡ 2. （圖片來源：網址 http://www.amazon.com ）

十分有名氣 Endless 鞋也被亞馬遜收購，在旗下購物平台販售

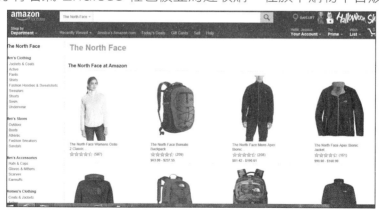

➡ 3. （圖片來源：網址 http://www.amazon.com）

美國嬰幼兒早期教育品牌 LeapFrog，在亞馬遜也有販售。

Part 1 教學篇

Part 2 商品篇

Part 3 旅遊篇

➡ **4.**（圖片來源：網址 http://www.amazon.com）

極地保暖的 The North Face 亦在亞馬遜有銷售平台。

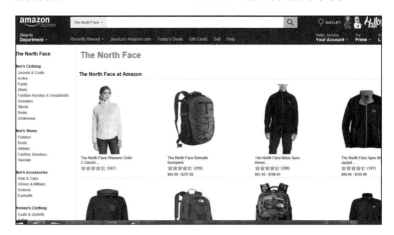

💟 小貼士

➢ 亞馬遜的網站因為操作容易，且有詳盡的流程説明。站上的商家眾
 多，甚至有百貨公司網路購物也設在此平台。因此，網購的初學者可
 以從亞馬遜開始研究，比較容易上手。

> 亞馬遜的商品有上萬種，以樂高來說，當您用 Lego 搜尋商品時，同一件商品，可能會出現不同的價格。因為賣家不同，或是商品條件不同（包裝，新舊），運送條件不同，而價格不同。您可以仔細閱讀好這些説明再做決定。 而如淘寶一樣，賣家有評分制，所以您也可以參考賣家們星等評價。

> 以上網站的資訊僅為參考，各個網站有時會出免費活動，或是更改運送規則。實際運費以您實際購物時，網站所公布的規則為準。

🎩 **Word Bank**

Movies, Music& Game 電影，音樂及遊戲	Toys,Kids & Beauty 玩具，兒童及美容
Electronics&Computers 電子產品&電腦產品	Clothing,Shoes& Jewelry 衣服，鞋子及珠寶
Home,Garden&Tools 家居，園藝及工具	Sports&Outdoors 運動及戶外
Beauty,Health&Grocery 美容，健康及雜貨	Automotive&Industrial 汽車及工業

Part 1 教學篇

Part 2 商品篇

Part 3 旅遊篇

11

實際操作
免運費篇

 實際操作

　　看完了前幾篇的教學,本篇要帶您操作一次購物流程,從 *免運費* 門檻低的網站介紹起。

情境對話

Christina: April, why Meredith is not in the office, there is an urgent shipping document, I need her signature on it.

April,為什麼 Meredith 不在辦公室,有份緊急的裝船文件要她簽名。

April: She told me that she will be in the office this afternoon, she has appointment with her dentist this morning.

她跟我説她下午才會進辦公室,早上她跟牙醫有約。

Christina: Ok, Then I can wait till

好吧,我可以等到下午。

this afternoon. Mr. Stephan needs those document urgently. The container is about to arrive Auckland, he can't clear the custom without those original shipping document. I had better call her and confirm the schedule with her.

Mr. Stephan 很需要這些文件，貨櫃就快到 Auckland 了，沒有正本文件不能清關。我最好還是打電話給 Meredith 跟她確認行程

April: Save the trouble, she is just coming in.

不用麻煩了，她正進辦公室呢。

Christina: Meredith, we thought you went to the dentist.

Meredith，我們以為你去牙醫那裏了。

Meredith: I did, it's just a scaling. It took shorter time than I expected.

去了呀，但是只是洗牙，比我預計的早結束。

Christina: Good, I need you to sign on those document.

太好了，我正需要你簽屬這些文件。

Meredith: Not a problem.

沒問題。

Christina: After I sending those document to Mr. Stephan, do you have a minute during the lunch time?

我把這文件寄給 Mr.Stephan 之後，可以借用你午餐時間嗎？不

Part 1 教學篇

Part 2 商品篇

Part 3 旅遊篇

It won't take long.

會很久。

Meredith: Well,I can skip the lunch . I had late breakfast, but why?

我早餐吃得晚,午餐可以跳過,但是有什麼事呢?

Christina: Apparently, April is the expert of online shopping now. She got many stuff in competitive price online. I wondered if you could demonstrate how to shop on international website for me.

很顯然的,April 現在是網購的專家,她買了許多好東西而且價格好優惠。我在想你是不是可以教我一下國際網購是如何操作的。

Meredith: Ok, as soon as I finish my work, I meet you in cafeteria.

好的,我把上午的工作完成之後,就到餐廳跟你碰面。

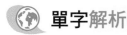 **單字解析**

Schedule [ˋskɛdʒʊl] *n./v.* 行程
例 The president's schedule is public.
→ 總統的行程是公開的。

句型解析

本書生活化的對話中為您介紹實用的句型或是短句，再舉例句說明，讓您看完之後，就能馬上輕鬆學會，不用背誦！！

Till...　直到…為止…

解 Till 可當介系詞或連接詞。分別例句為下；

例 They kept playing scooer till 6PM.

➡ 他們一直玩足球直到下午 6 點為止。

例 They kept playing scooer till the sun went down.

➡ 他們一直玩足球直到太陽下山為止。

as soon as　一怎樣…就怎樣

例 As soon as we arrive home, we start to prepare the dinner.

➡ 我們一回到家就開始準備晚餐

例 As soon as Ray finished school, her mom sent him back to Taiwan.

➡ Ray 一完成學業，他媽媽就送他回台灣。

 以上的單字及短句十分的簡單與實用，
讓您購物之餘，也能自然而然的學習英文哦。

Part 1 教學篇

Part 2 商品篇

Part 3 旅遊篇

◈ **相關網站】**（圖片來源：：網址 http://www.asos.tw ）

➡ **任務一：在 ASOS 找到一件女性參加婚禮的小禮服，品牌不限。**

Step1. 先將滑鼠移到 women 選項，即會出現相關商品

Step2. 點進 dresses 洋裝選項，選擇 dresses for wedding 婚禮洋裝。

Step3. 找到喜歡的洋裝，點選進去。

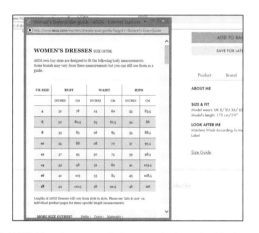

Step4. 找到洋裝的 size guide 尺寸表。根據自己三圍挑選尺寸。

Step5. 選擇好顏色，尺寸，將商品放入購物車 add to bag.

Step6. 加入成功之後，右上方購物車會出現我們的商品，再次確認好之後，選擇結帳 pay now會進入結帳畫面。

➡ **準備結帳**

Step1：點選 pay now 之後，直接進入信用卡資料填寫（見信用卡篇）寫完點選下一步 next step。

Step 2 進入確認付款 confirm & pay。開始核對訂單資料。

Step 3 選擇帳單地址是否跟運送地址相同。

Step 4 選擇是否要自費改成快遞，標準運送是免費的。

Step 5 核對信用卡資料，並輸入信用卡背後 3 碼。

Step 6 訂購完成。

 小貼士

➤ 對於網路購物的初學者可以先從網站有國際運送的服務開始，或是有低門檻免運的網站。以 ASOS 網站為例，有提供國際運送，免運門檻很低，一件洋裝（超過 NT1150）即可免運標準運送。可以在這類的大型網站先熟悉整個網購流程。

 Word Bank

Order Summary　訂單總結	Express　快遞
Select delivery & billing address 選擇運送&帳單地址	Select Payment Method 選擇付款方式
Delivery Option 運送選項	Enter Security Code 輸入安全號碼
Standard delivery　標準運送	

實際操作
需支付運費篇

🖥 操作實務篇

　　有些網站不論購物金額多少，國際客戶一律支付國際運費，使用國際快遞運送讓商品能夠更快、更安全的運送至客戶手中。

💎 情境對話

Christina: Meredith, over here. The spaghetti in the cafeteria is awful. You should skip it , but the coffee is good.

Meredith，這邊，自助餐廳的義大利麵味道好奇怪，你最好不要吃，不過咖啡還不錯。

Meredith: I'm not hungry anyway. April, <u>what brings you here</u>?

反正我也不餓，April，你怎麼來了。

April: I just met Christina, she mentioned that she was expecting you. If you don't mind I would like to join

我剛碰到 Christina，她說在這等你。如果你不介意的話，我可以加入嗎？

you.

Meredith: Don't be silly, we are just having girl's talk. I'm going to show Christina how to shop online, maybe you can share some experience with us.

別傻了，我們只是女生在聊天。問我怎麼上網購物的，我正要操作給她看。或許你可以跟我們分享你的經驗。

April: Me？I'm only the starter. I wouldn't show off in front of the true expert, don't make fun of me.

我？我才是個初學者。不敢在專家前賣弄，你不要笑我了。

Christina: Meredith, I bring my laptop. It will be easier to demonstrate. Let's start it.

Meredith，我把筆電帶來了，這樣你要操作比較容易，讓我們開始吧。

Meredith: Sure. What are you looking for exactly? It can narrow down the search range.

好呀。那你想找什麼產品呢？有產品可以縮小搜尋範圍。

Christina: You got me.That's a good question.

被你問倒了，這是個好問題。

Meredith: Without a specific item, it's kind of difficult to start it. You

沒有特定的項目，要開始有點困難。就你所知網路

know there are thousands website on internet. It would be time-saving if we can start from the item you are interested in. That's easy for you to remember the procedure.

上有上千個網站，如果我們可以從你有興趣的產品開始，比較節省時間，而你也容易將整個操作流程記下來。

Christina: In that case, I would like to buy a pair of snow boots , real UGG snow boots.

這樣的話，我想要買一雙雪靴，UGG 的雪靴。

 單字解析

procedure KK[prə`sidʒɚ] *n.* 程序

例 Before boarding, it's a normal procedure to check your belongings.

→ 登機前，檢查個人行李是一般的程序。

 句型解析

本書生活化的對話中為您介紹實用的句型或是短句，再舉例句說明，讓您看完之後，就能馬上輕鬆學會，不用背誦！！

1. what brings you here 什麼風把你吹來的

解 當我們在意料之外看到了某個朋友，想要問她怎麼來了，我們可以用 what brings you here？

例 A: Kelly, I thought you are in Denver, what brings you here?

B: I'm visiting my mom.

➤ A: Kelly，我以為你在 Denver，怎麼到這來了？

B: 我來看我媽媽。

2. In front of …… 在…之前

例 There is a mailbox in front of Daryl's house.

➤ Daryl 的房子前面有個信箱。

例 The girl in front of me was talking loudly on the phone.

➤ 我前面的女生講電話好大聲。

以上的單字及短句十分的簡單與實用，
讓您購物之餘，也能自然而然的學習英文哦。

◇ 相關網站

➤ **任務:在 UGG 買雙女經典短版雪靴，一雙小朋友的防水短靴。**

（圖片來源：網址 https://www.uggaustralia.com）

已在 UGG 網站註冊，建立好運送資料、帳單地址等。

Step 1. 先登入網站（見註冊篇），知道欲選購的尺寸（見尺寸篇）

Step 2. 在 Women 女鞋➤ Footwear 鞋子➤ Classic 經典款。
找到喜歡的短版雪靴，挑好，加入購物車 add to cart.

Step 3. 加入購物車之後，先不要選結帳 view cart and
checkout now。選擇旁邊的-繼續購物 continue shopping .

（圖片來源：網址 https://www.uggaustralia.com）

Step 4. 在 kids 童鞋▷ Boys 男童▷ New Arrivals 新到款式。找到喜歡的兒童防水雪靴，挑好顏色、尺寸，加入購物車 add to cart 之後，選結帳 view cart and checkout now。

➡ 進入結帳畫面

Step1. 若有 Coupon 折扣碼，請在 Enter Coupon 輸入折扣碼內輸入。

Part
1
教
學
篇

Part
2
商
品
篇

Part
3
旅
遊
篇

Step2. 選擇結帳 Checkout。

（圖片來源：網址 https://www.uggaustralia.com）

Step3. 因為之前登入已經建立好帳單&運送地址。Checkout 時便會自動跳出這些資料。並計算國際運費，UGG 的國際運費一律為 USD$75.0，自動加入。若尚未建立帳單&運送地址，可在此鍵入相關資料。

Step4. 帳單&運送地址確認好之後，下一步就是付款方式 Payment Methods.

Step5. 輸入持卡人姓名 Name on card，信用卡號 Number，
有效年月，安全碼 security code。若想儲存這張看片資
料，可按儲存卡片 Save this card。

Step6. 再次確認所有細節，完成訂購

 ## 小貼士

➤ 網站上常見的 Free shipping 免運費，通常是指美國免運。我們從國
外購物，請記得看 **International shipping** 國際運送這些單字。

➤ 通常網站上的 Sales Tax 營業稅為 0 是因為此項商品運到台灣，不
在美國境內銷售，所以營業稅為 0，不代表進口台灣時的營業稅為 0。

➤ 我們從國外網站購買超過美金 USD$100 就可能被台灣海關抽查到，
必須支付關稅、營業稅等。而國外網站，除非有特別強調結帳金額有
包含這些費用，表示貨物到您手上，無需再付任何費用。一般來說是
不包含的，以本篇 UGG 為例，網站上只收商品費用及運費。其他台
灣進口的關稅，營業稅則不含在內。（詳情請見關稅篇）

Word Bank

Model	款式	In stock	有庫存
View Cart	查看購物車	Checkout	結帳
Add to wishlist	加入購物清單	Payment Method	付款方式
Security Code	安全碼	Save this card	儲存這張卡片

Part 2
網購商品篇

🖥 設計女裝篇

　　越來越多人喜歡在網路上選購商品，除了快速與便捷之外，還有就是能搶先了解國外流行的趨勢，能滿足許多品味高雅的上班女性。

💎 情境對話

Meredith: Christina, you looks so tired, are you ok?

Christina，你看起來好累，還好吧?

Christina: No, on the contrary, there will be a new product launch party and the deadline is next Friday. Mer, you got to help me with that. I have no clue about those research and analysis data.

正好相反，我快完蛋了。新品發表會快到了，而且報告下週五之前要交。你一定要幫我，小梅，我真的對這些研究、分析數據一點頭緒也沒有。

Meredith: Sure thing. Let me see. It

沒問題，讓我看看。看來

seems that you had collected the relevant data. Now, all you have to do is clarifying those incoming data. Then you will get a final report. See, that's it.

你已經收集好相關資料了，現在你要做的是分類這些收集進來的資料，然後最後的報告就會出來了，你看，像這樣。

Christina: Wow, excellent report!! You won't believe how many hours I had spent last night. I just sit in front of my computer and can't figure out the next step. Now, I feel much relief.

哇，報告做得真好！！你不會相信我昨天花了幾個鐘頭在這上面，我就坐在電腦前面一籌莫展吶。現在我終於可以安心了。

Meredith: You should come to me earlier.

你應該早點來找我的。

Christina: I didn't want to call you in the middle of night.

我不想大半夜的打電話給你。

Meredith: Well, you can text first.

你可以先發簡訊給我呀。

Christina: Good idea, hey, have you met with the new girl yet, The manager assigned her in our department.

有道理！嘿，你有看到新來的女生嗎？經理將她分派到我們部門。

Part
1
教學篇

Part
2
商品篇

Part
3
旅遊篇

Meredith: No, have you? That's a good news. We could really need some extra help; otherwise, it's impossible to finish all those work by only two of us.

沒有，你見到她了嗎？這倒是個好消息，我們真的需要多個人手，不然光靠我們二個根本做不完這麼多事的。

Christina: Well, she looks very professional in that expensive dress.

那昂貴的套裝讓她看起來格外專業。

 單字解析

Analysis KK[ə`næləsɪs] *n.* 分析

例 Sandra's analysis is very objective. We should take her advice.

➔ Sandra 的分析十分客觀，我們應該聽從她的建議。

句型解析

 本書生活化的對話中為您介紹實用的句型或是短句，再舉例句說明，讓您看完之後，就能馬上輕鬆學會，不用背誦！！

I have no clue 我一點頭緒也沒有

解 當我們忙得一團亂，卻又一點進展也沒有，或是對於一件棘手的事件不知道該如何解決時，就可使用此句。

例 The manager asked Frank to submit the sales report, but

he has no clue about it.

➡ 經理要 Frank 交業績報告，但是他一點頭緒也沒有。

例 Their anniversary is coming, but Kevin has no clue about the gift.

➡ 他們的結婚紀念日快到了，但 Kevin 還是不知道要送什麼禮物。

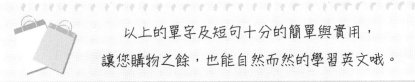

以上的單字及短句十分的簡單與實用，
讓您購物之餘，也能自然而然的學習英文哦。

相關網站

➡ **Ann Taylor**（圖片網址 http://www.anntaylor.com/）

網頁介紹：網站以台幣計價，美國女性上班族的時尚品牌。

國際運送：滿 US175，即可享 US19.95 標準運送台灣，關稅預付。

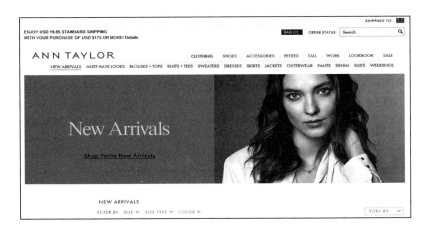

→ Loft（圖片網址：http://www.loft.com/）

網頁介紹：是 Ann Taylor 的年輕品牌，價格稍優惠，台幣計價。

國際運送：滿 US175，即可享 US19.95 標準運送台灣，關稅預付。

→ BCBG（圖片網址：http://www.bcbg.com）

網頁介紹：時尚高級女裝，網頁有部分中文簡介。

國際運送：Borderfree 運送，滿台幣 NT6100 享免運寄送台灣。

➡ **DKNY**　（圖片網址：http://www.dkny.com）

網頁介紹：Donna Karan New York 簡稱為知名的紐約時尚品牌
國際運送：透過 Borderfree 運送，任何美國境外訂單皆轉由
Borderfree 處理。

➡ **Rebecca Minkoff**

（圖片網址：http://www.rebeccaminkoff.com）

網頁介紹：名人都愛的 Rebecca Minkoff
國際運送：有送台灣，訂單超過 USD$300 免運費。

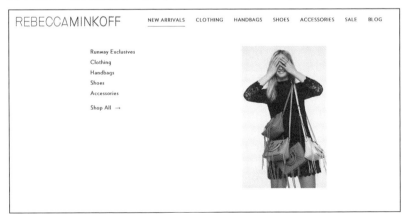

➡ **All Saints** （圖片網址：http://www.armaniexchange.com）

網頁介紹：來自英倫的時尚品牌

國際運送：訂單滿£250 享免費運送台灣，訂單不滿£250，運送台灣運費為£14.95

 小貼士

> All Saint 的折扣有時候多會到 50%，實在很划算。喜歡該品牌的朋友可以在換季時到官網看看。

> BCBG 的國際運送是與 borderfree.com 公司合作。另外與 borderfree 合作的商家也不少，您可以直接到 borderfree 網站上去了解進一步的流程。

> 在台灣給人高價印象的 Rebecca Minkoff 其實在官網上常有折扣商品，手提袋有時低至 40%off，再搭配註冊即享 15%的折扣碼十分划算。

➤ 以上網站的運費資訊僅為參考，各個網站有時會出免費活動，或是更改運送規則。實際運費以您實際購物時，網站所公布的規則為準。

Word Bank 女裝

Lace dress	蕾絲洋裝	Wrap dress	V 型包覆洋裝
Office to after hours	辦公&聚會	Cocktail dress	小禮服
Casual	休閒	Gowns dress	長禮服
Work	工作	Dresses	洋裝
Prints	印花	View all	查看所有
Sweaters	毛衣	Maxi dress	長洋裝
Tops	上衣	Skirts	裙子
Jumpsuit	連身褲	Jackets	外套
Leather	皮衣	Sale	折扣
Runway	休閒	Outerwear	外出服
Shoes	鞋	Accessories	配件
Bags	包	Pants	褲子
Jewelry	飾品	Fragrance	香水
Hats	帽子	Scarves	圍巾
Sunglasses	太陽眼鏡	Hair Accessories	髮飾
Belts	皮帶		

Unit 2
折扣精品
時尚品牌

💎 折扣精品

在正式的場合中，衣著不能馬虎。本篇介紹您國外的精品折扣網站，讓您以更輕鬆的價格，也能享有國際精品。

💎 情境對話

Meredith: Christina, the new product launch was very successful last night. Your presentation was quite impressive, good job.

Christina，昨天的新品發表會十分的成功，你的介紹十分讓人讓人印象深刻，做得好。

Christina: Thanks, but you did the hard work, not me. I stood in front of <u>a bunch of</u> reporters and talked only. You are the one who finished all the report and research. I can't accomplish it without your support.

謝啦，但是你才是幕後功臣，我沒做什麼事。我只是站在一群記者前說話，而你完成了所有的研究跟報告。沒有你，這件事就無法完成。

Meredith: You flatter me immensely. Don't be silly. We are a team. Besides, I don't know how to talk in front of people. I get nervous on such occasion. I bet you don't want me to ruin the new product launch, right ?

你實在太抬舉我了，別傻了，我們是互相幫忙。此外，我真的不知道怎麼樣在一群人面前說話。這種人多的場合，總是讓我很緊張。你不想新品發表會被我毀了吧。

Christina: Ha, you won't. Practice makes perfect. I have faiths in you.

你才不會呢。多練習就好了，我對你有信心的。

Meredith: Maybe, I would try next time. Speaking of next presentation. The manager have already arranged it. I just got the notice.

或許下次我來試試看。說到下次的發表會，經理已經安排好了，我剛收到通知。

Christina: When is it?

是什麼時候？

Meredith: Feb 16th. Right after the Chinese New Year.

2 月 16 日。剛好過農曆年後。

Christina: Well, then I guess we will have a lot of work to do before that.

那我們在這之前有好多工作必須完成。

Meredith: Relax, we will be well-pre-

放心，我們會為此作好充

pared for the presentation.

分準備的。

Christina: One more thing, I have to get some decent dresses for the press conference. Anything you recommend?

還有一件事,我還要找一些適合的洋裝出席記者會,有什麼推薦的嗎?

Meredith: Well, there are many discount designer dresses online. Maybe you can shop online.

網路上有許多折扣的設計師洋裝,或許你可以在網路上購物。

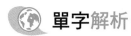 **單字解析**

Conference [ˋkɑnfərəns] *n.* **會議**

例 The conference was cancelled because of typhoon.

➡ 會議因為颱風而取消

句型解析

 本書生活化的對話中為您介紹實用的句型或是短句,再舉例句說明,讓您看完之後,就能馬上輕鬆學會,不用背誦!!

a bunch of 一群、堆

解 中文裡的量詞十分複雜,名詞不同所對應的量詞就不一樣,如:一束花,一串葡萄,一群人等等。常常讓外國朋友一頭霧水,因為在英文裡,一堆、一群物品的量詞都可以用 a bunch of 如

A bunch of flowers　　一束花

A bunch of grapes　　一串葡萄

A bunch of people　　一群人

例 There are a bunch of reporters in the conference room now. You should not go there.

➡ 現在會議室裡有一群記者，你最好不要去那裏。

例 Mom bought a bunch of grapes. You should have some.

➡ 媽媽買了些葡萄，你應該吃一點。

以上的單字及短句十分的簡單與實用，
讓您購物之餘，也能自然而然的學習英文哦。

相關網站

➡ **Bluefly**（圖片網址：http://www.bluefly.com）

網頁介紹：有許多時尚精品，亦有折扣。

國際運費：有運送台灣，結帳時運費及關稅等一同結算。

Part 1 教學篇

Part 2 商品篇

Part 3 旅遊篇

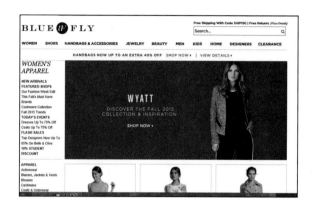

➡ **Yoox** （圖片網址：www.yoox.com）

網頁介紹：誰説精品不能平價，Yoox 就有許多折扣精品。

國際運送：滿美金$350 即享免費運送台灣，關稅等費用可預付。未滿 USD$350，運費 USD$26，走快遞。

➡ **Gilt** （圖片網址：http://www.gilt.com）

網頁介紹：有名的限時折扣精品店，自動翻譯中文網頁，台幣計價。

國際運費：訂單滿$100，運費 USD$9.95 運送台灣

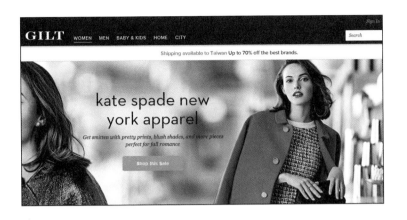

➡ **Hautelook**（圖片網址：http://www.hautelook.com）

網頁介紹：Nordstrom 百貨的折扣網站。

國際運費：沒有運送台灣，可透過代運公司運送。

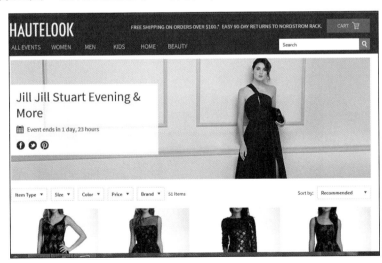

➡ **Ted Baker**（圖片網址：http://www.tedbaker.com）

網頁介紹：英國的設計師品牌，屬於中高價位，女裝與包包十分出色

國際運送：有送台灣，採快遞運送。依訂單重量決定運費。

Part 1 教學篇

Part 2 商品篇

Part 3 旅遊篇

➡ **Paul Smith** （圖片網址：http://www.paulsmith.co.uk）

網頁介紹：英國的設計師品牌，以男裝起家，現男女裝都有。

國際運送：有送台灣，運費£30，採標準運送，7-10 天到貨

💗 **小貼士**

➢ 這些限時折扣的網站透過電子郵件的方式告訴會員，何種商品於某會

於何時開始折扣。

➤ Hautelook 除了限時搶購之外，還有邀請朋友可得 USD$20 折價的活動。

➤ Gilt 的快閃特賣十分出名，亦有詳盡的中文網頁解釋國際運送問題及產品問題等，網購剛入門的朋友可以在 Gilt 網站上開始研究。

➤ 其中 Paul Smith 也出了童裝，從小嬰兒到 16 歲的青少年服飾都有。其設計帶有濃烈的英倫風，十分有質感。

➤ 以上網站的運費資訊僅為參考，各個網站有時會出免費活動，或是更改運送規則。實際運費以您實際購物時，網站所公布的規則為準。

🎩 Word Bank

Fall Boutiques	秋日精品	Designers	設計師系列
Rising Stars	明日之星	Must Have Brands	必買品牌
Today's Events	今日特賣	Flash Sales	快閃特價
10% student Discount 10% 學生特價		Free Shipping Cod 免運費折價代碼	

Unit 3

包包&好鞋

越來越多的女生重視配件的時尚設計，與衣著的搭配等。想找好看又時尚的包包與鞋子?請看本篇!

💎 情境對話

Christina: Meredith, I just got email from Mr. Keith. He would like to meet with you in Shanghai next month.

Meredith，Keith 先生剛寫封電子郵件來。他想要下個月在上海跟你會面。

Meredith: Shanghai ? Mr. Keith is from South Africa, why he wants to go to Shanghai? Did he mention any particular reason?

上海?Keith 先生是南非的客戶，為什要去上海，他有說什麼特別原因嗎?

Christina: Yes, for the Shanghai Tire show. It will start from 10/25-10/31. He would like to attend the show.

有，他要去參加上海輪胎展，從 10/25-10/31。

Meredith: I never heard of it. Are you sure?

我沒聽過這展覽，你確定嗎？

Christina: Yes, I also confirmed the information. It's the first year of Shanghai Tire Show. It just starts from this year.

沒錯，我剛也查過資料了。這是上海輪胎展的第一年，今年才開始的。

Meredith: Ok, then I bet we should attend the show as well.

好吧，我想我們應該也要去參加這展覽的。

Christina: Ok, I'll reply to Mr. Keith that you will meet with him in Shanghai.

那麼我會跟 Keith 回覆說你下個月會去上海跟他碰面。

Meredith: One more thing, please get your travel documents ready. You are going with me.

還有一件事，麻煩把你的證件準備好，你跟我去。

Christina: Am I?

我也要去嗎？

Meredith: What's wrong? Aren't you interested in Tire Show?

怎麼了嗎？你難道不想看看輪胎展嗎？

Christina: Yes, I am. And my travel

我想去看輪胎展，而且我

document is ready as usual.

的證件一直都準備好的。

Meredith: Then, what's the problem?

那是有什麼問題呢？

Christina: Remember last time we were in Beijing. My suitcase got broken. I still don't have time to buy a new one. You know, we have been so busy since last month.

記得上次去北京的時候，我行李摔壞了，一直沒有時間去買新的。你知道我們從上個月起就很忙。

Meredith: Don't worry. You will find a perfect one online.

別擔心，你會在網路上找到一個很棒的！

 單字解析

Reply [rɪ`plaɪ] *v./ n.* 回覆

例 Derek hasn't gotten the reply from Meredith. Maybe she doesn't want to go to the party at all.

→ Derek 還沒有得到 Meredith 的回覆，或許她根本不想去那派對。

Document [`dɑkjəmənt] *n.* 文件

例 We need the shipping document. Please send it ASAP.

→ 我們需要出貨文件，請盡快寄出。

句型解析

本書生活化的對話中為您介紹實用的句型或是短句，再舉例句說明，讓您看完之後，就能馬上輕鬆學會，不用背誦！！

S +would like to 想要（客氣的表達方式）

解 以此句型 I would like to 是英文用法裡一種極為客氣的表達。比直接的 I want to 我想要，來得客氣許多。

例 I would like to make a reservation for tomorrow dinner.

➜ 我想要為明天晚餐訂位。

例 If possible, I would like to cancel my flight.

➜ 如果可以的話，我想要取消我的航班。

S + never heard of it 從未聽過

例 I never heard of With company before, they must be a new company.

➜ 我之前從沒聽過 With 公司，他們應該是新公司吧！

例 It's such a scandal, we had never heard of it.

➜ 這真是個我們從未聽過的醜聞。

以上的單字及短句十分的簡單與實用，
讓您購物之餘，也能自然而然的學習英文哦。

相關網站

➡ **SHOPBOP** （圖片網址：https:// www.shopbop.com）

網站介紹：亞馬遜旗下的時尚網站，集結各大名牌，非常好逛！

國際運送：100 美元以上免運，低於 100 美元運費美金 10 美元。

➡ **eBags** （圖片網址：https://www.ebags.com）

網站介紹：美國最大的包包購物網站，網羅各大時尚，年輕品牌。

國際運費：透過 borderfreer 寄送，可以台幣計價。

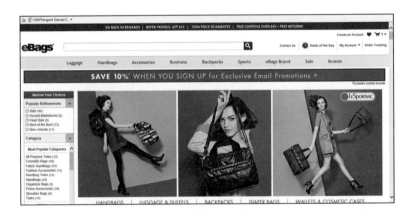

➡ **Cambridge satchel**（圖片網址：www.cambridgesatchel.com）

網站介紹：最流行的劍橋包英國官網

國際運費：可寄送，但沒有免運費門檻。寄到台灣費率有£14.99 - $23.99 - €20.99 - ¥148 四階。可直接去信客服，會根據訂單為您計算實際運費。

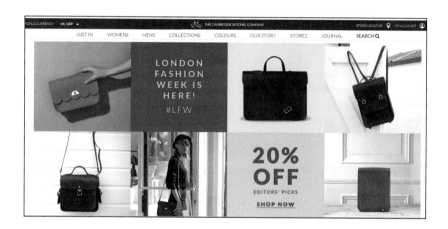

➡ **Aerosoles**（圖片來源：網址 http://www.aerosoles.com/store）

網頁介紹：從休閒鞋到靴子一應俱全。

國際運送：有運送台灣，走 UPS。

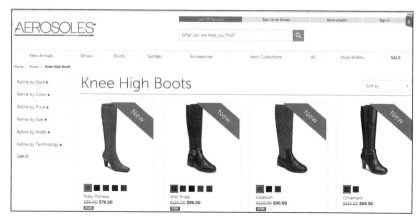

Part 1 教學篇

Part 2 商品篇

Part 3 旅遊篇

➡ **UGG**（圖片來源：網址 http://www.uggaustralia.com）

網頁介紹：最受女性歡迎的澳洲 UGG 雪靴

國際運送：有寄送國際，走 UPS，不論訂單金額，寄到台灣運費一律 USD$75。

➡ **Native**（圖片來源：網址 http://nativeshoes.com/）

網頁介紹：來自加拿大的新品牌，以輕便，色彩多樣大受歡迎。

國際運送：有寄送台灣，結帳時會計算運費跟進口關稅。

愛買小貼士

➤ SHOPBOP 另有推出介紹朋友加入會員，可得$25 購物金。網站裡也常有 SALE 折扣。喜歡撿便宜的消費者可先從 SALE 區尋寶。

➤ 喜歡劍橋包的人也可試試大陸的天貓網站，在天貓有官方授權的直購網站。若是有親友在大陸，可託買以節省運送費用。

➤ 以上網站的運費資訊僅為參考，各個網站有時會出免費活動，或是更改運送規則。實際運費以您實際購物時，網站所公布的規則為準。

Word Bank 各式樣包包怎麼說

Baby Bags	媽媽包	Cross Body Bags	斜背包
Backpacks	後背包	Hobos	弧形單肩背包
Beach Bags	海灘包	Luggage	行李箱
Black Handbags	黑色手拿包	Mini Bags	迷你包
Bucket Bags	水桶包	Satchels	方形公事包
Clutches	手拿包	Shoulder Bags	肩包
Cosmetic Pouches	化妝包	Wallets	皮夾
Totes	托特包		

女生就愛買衣服

💎 情境對話

Meredith: <u>As you can see</u>, after adding your favorite item in a shopping cart, the next step is check out. That's it.

就像你看到的，把你喜歡的商品加入購物車之後，然後你就可以結帳，這麼簡單。

Christina: Wow, apparently that's easier <u>than I expected</u>. How can I never thought about online shopping?

哇，很明顯的，這比我預料之中要簡單許多。我之前怎麼都沒有想過要網路購物。

Meredith: Hey, We are going to Hokkaido this winter, I wondered if I could add a pair of boots in the cart. I want to buy snow boots for my son. I'll spilt the freight and the tariff with you.

嘿，我們這個冬天要去北海道。我在想可不可以跟你一起買雙鞋，我想給我兒子買雙雪靴。運費跟關稅我們平分。

Christina: No problem. That will be more economical for me as well.

沒有問題。這樣我也會比較省錢。

April: Wow, there are so many choices online, they even have waterproof boots. That's perfect for Hokkaido.

哇，線上有好多選擇。甚至有防水的靴子，穿去北海道正好。

Meredith: You know my son. He is so excited about the Hokkaido trip. He loves snow. I bet he would love this boots.

你也知道我兒子的，他要去北海道他很開心，他很喜歡雪的。我猜他也一定會喜歡這靴子的。

April: Those are the latest designs, can I get one pair of those with you, too?

這些都是最新款！我可以也買一雙嗎？

Christina: Even better, now we can spilt the freight and tariff in 3.

再好也不過了，現在有三個人平分運費跟關稅了。

April: Thanks, you know what, some websites show how celebrities dress up. I usually check those information before shopping online. It's easy to follow the fashion trend. Those latest

謝謝你，你知道嗎？有些網站會告訴你名人怎麼打扮的。在購物前我都會先去看看這些資訊。這些比較容易掌握流行趨勢，這

designs are really popular now, many celebrities wear those boots.

些最新款真的很受歡迎，好多名人都穿。

🌐 單字解析

Waterproof [`wɔtɚˌpruf] *adj/v./n.* 防水的

例 I don't need raincoat. This jacket is waterproof.

➜ 我不需要雨衣，這外套是防水的

Popular [`pɑpjələ] *adj* 受歡迎的

例 Star Wars is a very popular American movies.

➜ 星際大戰是很受歡迎的美國電影。

📱 句型解析

本書生活化的對話中為您介紹實用的句型或是短句，再舉例句說明，讓您看完之後，就能馬上輕鬆學會，不用背誦！！

As you can see 如你所見

解 當我們帶領別人參觀，或是展示過某事之後，我們要再提起此事，就可用 As you can see, 如你所見，作為開頭。

例 As you can see, it's a beautiful house. Your family would love it.

➜ 如你所見，這是間漂亮的房子，你的家人會喜歡的。

例 As you can see, the typhoon had caused those damage.

➜ 如你所見，颱風造成這些損失。

than I expected …超過我的期望

解 這是放在句尾的句型，前面要加比較級的句子。

例 The food here is much better than I expected.

➜ 這裡的食物比我想像的好吃。

例 The traffic is worse than I expected.

➜ 交通比我想像的還要糟。

以上的單字及短句十分的簡單與實用，

讓您購物之餘，也能自然而然的學習英文哦。

💎 相關網站

➜ **Intermix** （圖片來源：網址 http://www.intermixonline.com/）

網頁介紹：女性時尚新品牌。

國際運送：有寄送台灣，台灣關稅等進口費用結帳時結算，台幣計價。

➡ Black label Boutique

（圖片來源：網址 http://www.blacklabelboutique.com/ ）

網頁介紹：許多年輕女生喜歡的品牌。

國際運送：沒有寄送台灣，可找代運公司運送。

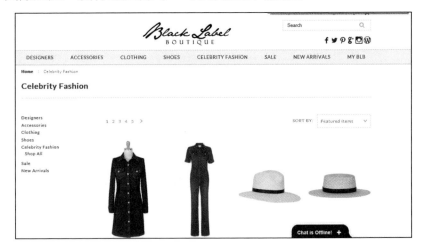

➡ Boutique To You

（圖片來源：網址 https://www.boutiquetoyou.com）

網頁介紹：時尚品牌，還有許多名人穿搭介紹。。

國際運送：有寄送台灣，運費 USD$35.00，帳單地址與運送地址需一致售價不含台灣關稅等進口費用。

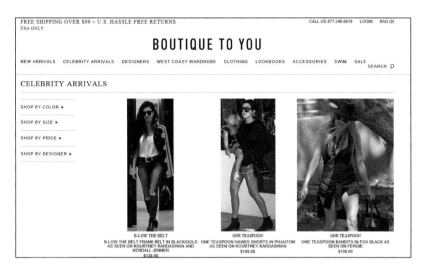

➡ **NASTY GAL** （圖片來源：網址 http://www.nastygal.com）

網頁介紹：從復古經典服飾躍升成為知名品牌。

國際運送：有寄送台灣，標準運送運費 US$15.0 快遞運送運費

USD$49.0。售價不含台灣關稅等進口費用。

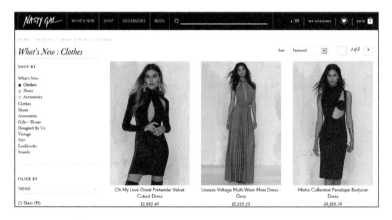

➡ **Marks and Spencer**

（圖片來源：網址 http://www.marksandspencer.com/）

網頁介紹：英國知名的馬莎百貨也有網購

國際運送：有寄送台灣，標準運送英鎊 £$15.0。售價不含台灣關稅等進口費用

➡ The Outnet

（圖片網址：http: https://www.theoutnet.com/en-TW/）

網頁介紹：Net A Porter 的 outlet 網站，台幣計價

國際運送：有運送台灣，運費為£24.00 採快遞運送。

小貼士

➤ 馬莎百貨雖然商品齊全，但是僅有衣服及家飾提供運送國際。購物前請先看清楚網站的寄送規則。

➤ 在網購之前，請先稍微研究您要的購物網站。盡量選擇大型，知名正當營業的網站。大型的購物網站，客戶服務支援較為完善即時。若商品有瑕疵要辦理退貨，也能得到即時迅速的服務。

➤ 有些品牌因為太受歡迎，可能在您搜尋該品牌時，會出現許多類似官網的網站，請慎選。網路購物，首重網路安全，而非商品價格。盡量找該品牌的官網，或是知名的大型購物購物網站，避免選上來路不明的網站購物。

➤ 以上網站的運費資訊僅為參考，各個網站有時會出免費活動，或是更改運送規則。實際運費以您實際購物時，網站所公布的規則為準。

Word Bank

Latest trend	最新流行	Best Sellers	暢銷商品
Vintage	復古	Gift cards	禮物卡
Party Wear	派對穿著	Sportswear	運動穿著
Lingerie	內衣		

Part 1 教學篇

Part 2 商品篇

Part 3 旅遊篇

精品購物網站介紹

💎 購物網站

網路購物讓人看得眼花撩亂，不知上哪個網站嗎？本篇介紹高級網路網站，其商品內容有設計女裝、鞋子等，一次滿足所有的購物需求。

💎 情境對話

Meredith: Good morning, April, you look exhausted. Are you ok? Did you try to finish the quarterly progress report last night?

早安，April，你看起來很累，你還好嗎？是不是昨晚在趕每季銷售進度報告？

April: Ha！I already finished it last week, and submitted it to the general manager. It turns out that we have reached our sales goal successfully. The economy prosperity is much better than we expected.

嘿！我上週就完成而且交給總經理了。結果我們成功地達成銷售目標，經濟景氣比我們預期的要好很多。

Meredith: Well, good to hear that. Then why you look so tired?

嗯，這是個好消息。那你怎麼看起來很累？

April: The general manager promised that we could have extra bonuses if the sales goal is achieved. Now, we made it. So I would like to buy something nice to reward myself.

總經理答應過，如果我們銷售目標能達成，就能有筆額外的獎金。現在，我們辦到了，所以我想給自己買些好東西獎勵自己。

Meredith: What do you want to buy?

你想買什麼呢？

April: Some dresses, shoes, and a pair of sunglass, I really need sunglass when I driving. The sun is always in my eyes, I can hardly see. You know how dangerous it can be. So, I spent hours online last night searching those items.

幾件洋裝、一雙鞋跟一副太陽眼鏡。開車的時候，我真的很需要太陽眼鏡。眼睛總是張不開，你知道這樣開車有多危險吧！所以昨天我花了好幾個鐘頭在網路上找這些東西。

Meredith: Did you find anything you like?

你有找到喜歡的嗎？

April: Yes, I did. But these items are from different websites. It's kind of

有的，但是都是在不同網站上看到的，這樣有點麻

trouble.	煩吶～。
Meredith : Well, you know there are some websites.They have everything you need, such as clothing, shoes, and accessories for both woman and man. You can shop on those websites. It's quite convenient.	你知道有些網站他們有許多產品。你想買的，像是衣服、鞋和配件等，男生的女生的都有。相當方便吶！
April: Really？Show me！！	真的嗎？秀給我看！

🌐 單字解析

Quarterly [`kwɔrtəlɪ] *ad.* 每季的

例 The school paper is published quarterly.

➜ 校刊每季發行

💲 句型解析

本書生活化的對話中為您介紹實用的句型或是短句，再舉例句說明，讓您看完之後，就能馬上輕鬆學會，不用背誦！！

It turns out that　原來

解 1: 該句是用在我們本來期望某件事會發上，後來並沒有。與預期相反的情況出現時，可以使用 it turns out that….

例 Kelly didn't show up yesterday. It turned out she was sick then.

➜ Kelly 昨天沒有來，原來她那時候病了！

解 2 或是我們後來意外發現了某件事，也可以使用 it turns out that

例 Derek doesn't eat shrimp. It turns out that he is allergic to seafood.

➜ Derek 不吃蝦，原來他對海鮮過敏。

We made it　我們辦到了

解 當我們完成某項目標時，最口語、簡潔的句型就是 We made it. 或是再簡單一點，We did it. !!!

例 You should be proud of yourself. We made it.

➜ 我們辦到了！你應該覺得很自豪。

以上的單字及短句十分的簡單與實用，
讓您購物之餘，也能自然而然的學習英文哦。

💎 相關網站

➜ **Nordstrom** （圖片網址 http://shop.nordstrom.com/）

　　網頁介紹：美國的高級百貨 Nordstrom 的線上網站，貴婦的最愛。選擇地區之後以台幣計價。國際運送：透過 borderfree 寄送台灣服務。關稅跟營業稅可在結帳時預付。

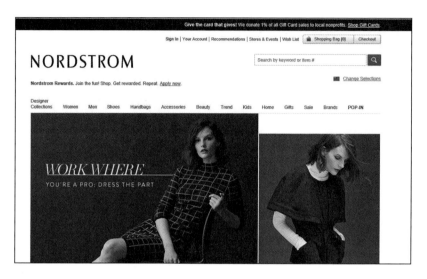

➡ **Sakes Fifth Avenue** （圖片網址 http://www.saksfifthavenue.com）

網頁介紹：紐約的高級百貨 Sakes Fifth Avenue 的線上網站。

國際運送：訂單超過美金 USD100，運費 USD$20，採標準運

送。商品售價以台幣計價，關稅跟營業稅可在結帳時預付。

➡ **Neiman Marcus** （圖片網址 http://www.neimanmarcus.com）

網頁介紹：美國的高級百貨龍頭 Neiman Marcus 的線上網站。

國際運送：透過 borderfree 寄送，免國際運費門檻 USD$175，採標準運送。關稅跟營業稅可選擇在結帳時預付。

➡ **Net-A-Porter** （圖片網址：http://www.net-a-porter.com）

網頁介紹：來自英國的奢侈品高級時尚網站，最好的時尚精品都在這裡。有推出中文網頁，但以美金計價。

國際運送：寄送至台灣地區運費 USD$15.約 2-3 天到貨

Part 1 教學篇

Part 2 商品篇

Part 3 旅遊篇

➡ **Mytheresa** （圖片網址：http://www.mytheresa.com）

網頁介紹：來自歐洲的奢侈品高級時尚網站

國際運送：DHL 寄送至台灣地區運費 USD$69.約 2-5 天到貨。

➡ **Barneys New York** （圖片網址：http://www.barneys.com/）

網頁介紹：奢侈品高級時尚網站。

國際運送：有送台灣，運費結帳跟關稅等一起算。美國境內免運。

購物小貼士

➤ 高級百貨的網站如 Sakes Fifth Avenue 及 Neiman Marcus，提供的商品多為當季現貨，品牌多，選擇也齊全，適合消費能力高的消費者。

➤ 如果想找折扣精品，則建議到 bluefly、Yoox、Gult 網站尋寶，有許多基本款都會做特價。

➤ 以上網站的運費資訊僅為參考，各個網站有時會出免費活動，或是更改運送規則。實際運費以您實際購物時，網站所公布的規則為準。

Word Bank 各式分類怎麼說

　　以上介紹的網站都是大型的綜合購物網站，先就首頁看到的大項分類列出單字。

Designer Collect	設計師系列	Clothing	服飾
New In	新貨到	Beauty	美容
Shoes	鞋子	Jewelry	珠寶
Brands	品牌	Kids	童裝
Trend	時尚	Men	男士系列
Home	家居	Bags&Accessories	包包與配件

💎 休閒服飾篇

休閒與運動兼顧時尚舒適，本篇要介紹在美國當地十分受歡迎的休閒及運動服飾，包含了平價與中高價系列。

💎 情境對話

Glenn: Hey, Maggie, did you study the calculus last night? Professor Hector said there will be a quiz this afternoon, chapter 2.

嘿，Maggie，你昨天有讀微積分嗎？Hector 教授說今天下午要考第二章。

Maggie: Are you kidding me? I don't remember it. When did he mention it? Are you sure?

你不是在開玩笑吧，我不記得有這件事，他什麼時候提起的？真的嗎？

Glenn: Last Friday, 10 mins before the class dismissed. He said that we

上週五，要下課前 10 分鐘，還說我們最好要充分

should get well prepared for the test. It may be related to our final report. <u>Does it ring a bell?</u>

準備好考試，成績有可能會記錄到學期末報告裡。有想起來嗎？

Maggie: No, I fell asleep then, that's pathetic.

沒有，我那時候睡著了，太可悲了！！

Glenn: I suggest that you study from now since I have already reminded you. There is still 5 hours before the test. You shouldn't give up.

既然我都提醒你了，我建議你現在開始讀，離考試還有 5 小時，不要放棄呀。

Maggie: You are absolutely right. But honest speaking, I didn't take notes in the class. Can I borrow yours? Please?

你說得很對，但是老實說，我沒有抄筆記，你的筆記可以借我嗎？拜託？

Glenn: Ok, here you are. Try to focus on the section 3. It's kind of tricky. I spent much time on this part last night.

沒問題，在這裡。重點在第 3 節，這裡有點難，我昨天在這裡花了很多時間。

Maggie: You are a lifesaver.

你真是幫我個大忙。

Glenn: Don't be silly. You have been

別傻了，你才幫我很多。

helping me so much. Remember the sweater you bought for me on-line. My sister really likes it. She said that she couldn't get such fashion design sweater here. You are very capable.

記得你上次在網路上幫我買的圓領衫嗎？我妹妹很喜歡這件衣服。她說這裡沒有這麼流行的款式，你真是很能幹。

Maggie: Well, I hope my calculus ability is good as well.

嗯，我希望我的微積分也一樣好呀！

 單字解析

Dismiss [dɪs`mɪs] *v.* 解散

例 The students were dismissed. They should focus on study not protest.

➡ 學生們被解散了，他們應該要好好讀書而不是花時間抗爭。

句型解析

 本書生活化的對話中為您介紹實用的句型或是短句，再舉例句說明，讓您看完之後，就能馬上輕鬆學會，不用背誦！！

Are you kidding me? 你開玩笑的吧！

解 說這句話時，表示不可置信，對於對方所說的訊息感到意外

例 A: Ivan is getting married next week.

B: Are you kidding me ?

➡ A: Ivan 下週要結婚了

B: 你開玩笑的吧？

Does it ring a bell? 有想起來嗎？

解 ring a bell 字面看來是敲鐘，引用為我們說的話，當別人想不起某事時，經過我們的提醒之後，聯想起來。

可用此句 Does it ring a bell, 有想起什麼嗎？

例 We went to Denmark last year, to LEGOLAND. Does it ring a bell ?

➜ 我們去年去丹麥，樂高樂園，記得嗎？

以上的單字及短句十分的簡單與實用，
讓您購物之餘，也能自然而然的學習英文哦。

◈ 相關網站

➡ **Abercrombie & Fitch**

（圖片網址：http://www.abercrombie.com）

網站介紹：時尚又年輕的美國知名品牌

國際運費：滿 NT5000 即免運，有中文網站，更方便選購！

➡ **Old Navy** （圖片網址：http://oldnavy.gap.com）

網站介紹：Gap 旗下平價休閒服飾

國際運費：透過 Borderfree 寄送國際，運費依訂單重量有所不同，結帳時結算。

➡ **J Crew** （網址：http:// www.jcrew.com）

網站介紹：中高價位的美國休閒服飾，十分受歡迎。台幣計價。

國際運費：有運送台灣，運費 NT830，採標準運送。

➡ **Under Armour** （圖片來源：網址 http://www.underarmour.tw）

網頁介紹：已超越 Adidas 成為第二大規模的運動品牌，中文網站。

國際運送：從中國寄送，走順豐快遞，運費台幣 NT200

➡ **LE COQ SPORTIF.SPORT**

（圖片來源：網址 http://www.lecoqsportif.com）

網頁介紹：來自法國的運動品牌，lego 有隻公雞

國際運送：有寄送台灣，採標準運送，運費為 14,90 歐元

⇒ **Lululemon** （圖片來源：網址 http://shop.lululemon.com）

網頁介紹：知名的瑜珈服裝專賣店。

國際運送：有送台灣，目前免運費。

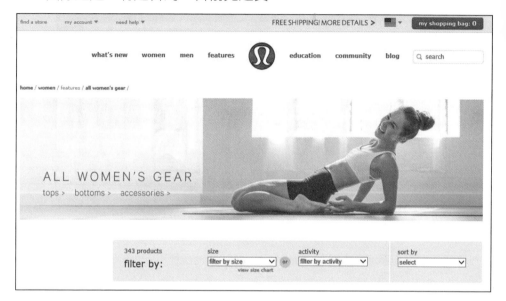

小貼士

➢ 依最新款的男鞋來說，在 Under Armour 美國網站的單價，跟中文網站的售價僅價差 10%。建議當季商品直接在中文網站購買。

➢ 東方人的身高一般來說較歐美人士嬌小，有些網站會推出 Petite 系列，給個子較小的人士，可以先從這系列看看是否有較合身的衣服。

➢ J crew 在首頁上都有網路專屬的最新的折扣碼，請記得看左上角的英文提示，在 use code（使用折扣碼）後面的就是最新的折扣碼。

> 以上網站的運費資訊僅為參考，各個網站有時會出免費活動，或是更改運送規則。實際運費以您實際購物時，網站所公布的規則為準。

🎩 Word Bank 常見的休閒服飾

Suiting	套裝	Sport coats	運動外套
dresses	洋裝	Outerwear	外套
Skirts	裙子	Blazers	西裝外套
Denim	牛仔褲	Vests	背心
Shorts	短褲	Tank Tops	坦克背心
Swim	泳裝	Hoodies	連帽上衣
Sleepwear	睡衣	Blouses	襯衫上衣
Pants	褲子	T-Shirts	一般休閒上衣
Intimates	內衣	Sweaters	圓領衫
Leggings	緊身褲	Shirts & Tops	襯衫上衣
Cardigans	開襟羊毛衫	Jumpsuits	連身褲
Polos	有領上衣	Sweatshirts	圓領衫

Unit 7
平價時尚網站

平價時尚

　　流行元素結合平價更能受到年輕旅群的喜愛，本篇要介紹的是一些平價購物網站，有十分知名的 ASOS 及 6PM 等。

情境對話

Glenn: Maggie, do you have any plan this afternoon?

Maggie，你今天下午有事嗎？

Maggie: Not really, I would stay in the dormitory and study the calculus. Why?

算不上什麼計劃，我會在宿舍念微積分，怎麼了嗎？

Glenn: Well, my sister is visiting. She wants to see you, if it's ok for you.

我妹妹來看我，但是如果可能的話，她想見見你。

Maggie: Me？Why？I'm not a celebrity. You should take her for sightseeing.

我？為什麼？我也不是什麼名人，你應該帶她到處看看的。

Glenn: In fact, she would like to thank you in person, after all, you had helped her so many times.

事實上，她想當面跟你道謝，畢竟你幫她好多次忙。

Maggie: You mean shopping online? That's really not a big deal, but I wouldn't mind meeting a new friend.

你是說在網路上購物嗎？那真的沒有什麼麻煩的，不過我願意多認識新朋友的。

Glenn: Thanks. I'll call you this afternoon.

謝啦，我下午打電話給你。

Glenn: Maggie, it's my sister, Beth. Beth, this is Maggie.

Maggie，這是我妹妹，Beth。Beth 這位是 Maggie。

Maggie: Hi, Beth, Glenn said that you are visiting. How is the trip? Have you seen the Taipei101?

嗨，Beth，Glenn 說你來玩，還愉快嗎？有去看過台北 101 了嗎？

Beth: Not yet, but I definitely will. I

還沒有，不過我一定會去

Part 1 教學篇

Part 2 商品篇

Part 3 旅遊篇

heard it's a terrific building. But I would like to meet you first. You are a big sister to me. Thanks for helping me so many times. I really appreciate it.

的，我聽説台北 101 是個很了不起的建築物。但是，我想先來見你，你就像我的大姊一樣，謝謝你幫了我許多次，真的很感激。

Maggie: No problem at all. I like shopping. You know I have 2 old brothers only. They don't like shopping, actually. They <u>can't stand it</u>. I'm glad that finally I have someone to share those information.

不要這麼客氣。我喜歡購物，你知道我只有二個哥哥。他們不喜歡買東西，事實上，他們很受不了我這樣。我很高興我終於可以分享我的購物經了。

🌐 單字解析

Dormitory [`dɔrmə͵torɪ] *n.* 宿舍

例 Carrie doesn't like the dormitory, so she moved out last week.

➡ Carrie 不喜歡宿舍，所以她上週搬出來了。

Sightseeing [`saɪt͵siɪŋ] *n.* 觀光

例 We spent a lot of time on sightseeing, not shopping.

➡ 我們大部分的時間都在觀光，而沒有購物。

句型解析

本書生活化的對話中為您介紹實用的句型或是短句，再舉例句說明，讓您看完之後，就能馬上輕鬆學會，不用背誦！！

Part 1 教學篇

S + can't stand it　受不了

解 Stand 的字面意思是站立，我們用 can't stand it 表示受不了。

例 The construction noise is so annoying. I can't stand it.

➔ 工程的噪音好煩人，我受不了。

例 Keith's girlfriend is so moody. He can't stand her.

➔ Keith 的女朋友喜怒無常，他受不了她。

Part 2 商品篇

以上的單字及短句十分的簡單與實用，

讓您購物之餘，也能自然而然的學習英文哦。

相關網站

Part 3 旅遊篇

➔ **ASOS**（圖片網址：http:// www.asos.com ）

網頁介紹：英國最大的時尚線上購物網站，有上萬品牌，亦有 ASOS 自創品牌。除了好買、好優惠之外，更有 outlet 商品等你挖寶！！

國際運送：標準運送 14 天內送達。超過 NT1150 免運，低於 NT1150 則需支付運費 NT175。快遞運送，4 天內到貨，運費 NT1350。

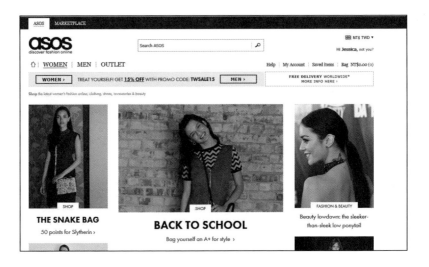

➡ **Marcy** （圖片網址：http://www1.macys.com/）

網頁介紹：美國線上購物網站，有上萬個品牌。

國際運送：透過 Borderfree 運送，運費於結帳時跟關稅等結算。

➡ 6 PM （圖片網址 http://www.6pm.com/）

網頁介紹：美國平價購物網站，有許多知名鞋款。

國際運送：美國境內免運，建議請代運公司運送。

➡ Country Attire （圖片網址 http://www.countryattire.com）

網頁介紹：英國的購物網站，好逛又有折扣。

國際運送：訂單滿英鎊£100 免運，3-14 天到貨。

⇒ **CHOIES** （圖片網址：www.choies.com）

網頁介紹：小資女的最愛，想要跟上流行，又不傷荷包。

國際運費：全球免運！！！！只要商品的左上角有秀出 FREE SHOPPING 表示免運費。您購買的商品只要含有一項免運費商品即可。一般運送約 11-16 天寄達。若您有急單，可支付快遞費 US$15,3-5 天送達。

⇒ **Revolve** （圖片網址：http://www.revolveclothing.com）

網頁介紹：有許多穿搭的介紹，讓購物更有靈感。

國際運費：滿 USD$100 享免費寄送台灣，採標準運送 10-15 天。

購物小貼士

➢ ASOS 為英國最大的線上購物網站，除了免運費之後，還有一項特別的服務就是可以看到模特兒實穿走秀展示衣服。選看商品時，記得要點選商品旁的 View catwalk 檢視實穿。如此消費者可以大概得知這洋裝穿出來是否適合自己。減少買錯退貨的機率。

➢ Choies 網站有個特色就是可以即時與客服人員對話，有點像是淘寶的即時對談。只要點選網站裡的 Livechat 填入電子郵件，姓名跟問題，就可以開始與客服人員對談。

➢ 以上網站的運費資訊僅為參考，各個網站有時會出免費活動，或是更改運送規則。實際運費以您實際購物時，網站所公布的規則為準。

Word Bank

New in	新貨到	Accessories	配件
Shoes	鞋子	Clearance	清倉
Clothing	衣服	Women's	女生系列
Bags	包包	Men's	男生系列
Kids'	兒童系列	Brands	品牌
Activities	活動		

Part 1 教學篇

Part 2 商品篇

Part 3 旅遊篇

Unit 8
英國平價品牌女裝

💎 平價服飾

　　平價服飾西班牙的 ZARA、瑞典的 H&M 到日本的 Uniqlo 都已進駐台灣。事實上，英國也有許多不錯的平價服飾，您在網路上就可購買。

💎 情境對話

Maggie: I'm so glad it's Friday. It's been a busy week, I really need some rest during the weekend.

終於星期五了，這週真的很忙。我週末要好好休息了。

Glenn: That sounds like a plan, but you can go out with us.

聽起來你都計畫好了。不過你可以跟我們出去玩。

Maggie: You ?

你們？

Glenn: Yes, listen, Beth and I are going to Taipei 101 tomorrow morn-

對呀，Beth 跟我明天早上要去台北 101，你要

ing. We wonder if you would like to join us. It will be fun.

不要跟我們一起去，會很好玩的。

Maggie: Well, I'm not sure if I have energy for that.

我不確定我是否有體力去 101 耶。

Glenn: Come on, it's weekend. You deserve having fun instead of staying in the dormitory. Beth really expects you to join us. Besides, you girls can talk all the way. Have you been to Taipei101? I got some coupons from a friend. It's only half price for the observatory ticket, don't you want to try the world's fastest elevator and see the wind damper? It's so famous.

拜託，週末耶。你應該要放鬆一下，而不是待在宿舍裡。Beth 很期待你能跟我們一起去。此外，你們女生最愛聊天了。你去過台北 101 嗎？我朋友給我折價券，到觀景台的票只要半價，難道你不想乘坐世界上最快的電梯？看看風阻球嗎？那很有名耶。

Maggie: you know sometimes, you are very persuasive.

你知道有時候，你蠻會說服別人的。

Glenn: I'm just telling the truth, even Hugh Jackman had been there. Hey, he is the wolverine.

我只是說出事實，連休傑克曼都去過 101，嘿！他是金鋼狼耶。

Part
1
教學篇

Part
2
商品篇

Part
3
旅遊篇

Maggie: Ok, <u>I heard you</u>. Where should I meet you tomorrow?

好好，我聽到了。那明天我們約哪裡碰面？

Glenn: 10 AM at Taipei station. You won't regret it. Beth said she would like to go to the mall. You girls love shopping, right ?

早上 10 點在台北車站。你不會後悔的。Beth 說她還想去商場逛逛，你們女生最喜歡逛街了。

🌐 單字解析

Observatory [əb`zɜ·vəˌtorɪ] *n.* 觀景台

例 Ivan refused to go to the observatory. He got acrophobia.

➜ Ivan 不想去觀景台，他有懼高症。

📋 句型解析

本書生活化的對話中為您介紹實用的句型或是短句，再舉例句說明，讓您看完之後，就能馬上輕鬆學會，不用背誦！！

Instead of 而不是

解 通常我們要表示某件事情應該是 A，而不是 B 時，可以用 instead of。

例 You should go to school instead of staying at home and doing nothing.

➜ 你應該去上學，而不是待在家裡無所事事。

例 They gave Mohammed some pieces of advice instead of

money.

➡ 他們給 Mohammed 一些建議，而不是提供他金錢。

I heard you 我聽到了

解 當對方不斷地陳述某項事情，我們可以說 I heard you 我聽到了。表達我們有收到對方所說的訊息，並且帶有，我聽到了，請不要再說了的隱意。

例 A: You should submit the final report before this Friday. The manager will need it to negotiate with client, are you listening to me？

B: Ok, I heard you.

➡ A：你在星期五前要將最後的報告交出來，經理需要這份報告跟客戶談判，有聽到我說的嗎？

　B: 好的，我聽到了。

以上的單字及短句十分的簡單與實用，
讓您購物之餘，也能自然而然的學習英文哦。

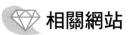 **相關網站**

➡ **TOPSHOP** （圖片網址：www.topshop.com）

　網頁介紹：來自英國最時尚的平價潮流品牌，亦有實體店面。

　國際運送：滿英鎊£100，則免運費£10.5，標準運送約 9 天到貨。

亦可支付快遞費£20，走國際快遞。

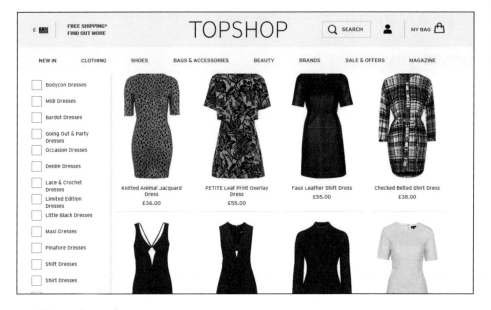

➡ **New Look** （圖片網址：http://www.newlook.com）

網頁介紹：英國平價女裝著名品牌。

國際運送：購物滿 £55 免運費運送台灣，採標準運送。

➡ **River land** （圖片網址：http://www.riverisland.com）

網頁介紹：十分受年輕人喜歡的英國潮流品牌，有實體店面

國際運送：運送台灣運費£10，採標準運送，約 10 天到貨。

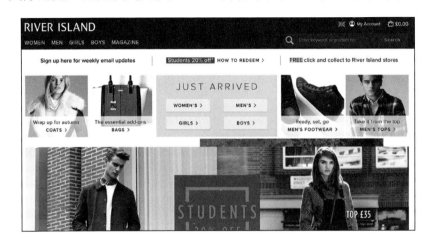

➡ **Dorothy Perkins** （圖片網址：http://www.dorothyperkins.com）

網頁介紹：價格優惠的時尚品牌

國際運送：運送台灣運費£10.5，採標準運送，約 8 天到貨。

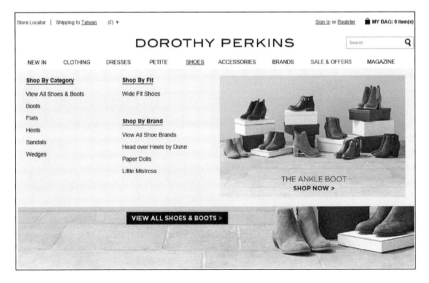

Part 1 教學篇

Part 2 商品篇

Part 3 旅遊篇

➡ **Warehouse** （圖片網址：http://www.warehouse.co.uk）

網頁介紹：流行都市風的潮流品牌

國際運送：運送台灣運費 US$25，採標準運送，約 10 天到貨。

➡ **Miss Selfridge** （圖片網址：http://www.missselfridge.com）

網頁介紹：帶點性感的平價品牌

國際運送：訂單滿 £50 享免費運送台灣，採標準運送。

小貼士

➤ 許多英國網站越來越國際化了，除了推出低門檻的免運費購物，甚至有的還推出中文網站。讓喜歡網路購物的消費者更是躍躍欲試。

➤ Topshop 香港跟日本也都有實體店面！喜歡這品牌的女生出國玩的時候，可以規劃一下行程到實體店面逛逛。另外，網站三不五時會推出限時所有訂單免運費，可以常上官網看看。

➤ 以上網站的運費資訊僅為參考，各個網站有時會出免費活動，或是更改運送規則。實際運費以您實際購物時，網站所公布的規則為準。

Word Bank

Shop by Category	以分類選購	Maternity	孕婦
Topshop design	獨享設計	Shop by Collection	以系列選購
Shop by Fit	以體型選購	Plus size	大尺碼
Tall	高個子	Teens	青少年
Petite	嬌小	Trend	流行趨勢

Part 1 教學篇

Part 2 商品篇

Part 3 旅遊篇

💎 美國平價服飾

　　美國平價女裝最著名的應該是 Forever 21，除了大家熟悉的 Forever 21，本篇另外介紹一些在當地十分受到年輕女性喜歡的平價服飾。

💎 情境對話

Beth: Maggie, over here.

Maggie，我們在這邊。

Maggie: Sorry that I'm late. I forgot to set the alarm last night.

抱歉，我遲到了。昨天忘記調鬧鐘了。

Beth: Don't worry. We just got here. Glenn is not familiar with this area. It took us a while to get the right direction and the traffic was really bad .

沒關係，我們也才剛到。這區 Glenn 不熟，我們花了點時間找路，而且路上交通好亂吶。

Glenn: I'm starving, can we have breakfast first? I just glanced at the station, there are so many fancy restaurants upstairs.

我快餓扁了，可以先吃早餐嗎？我瞄了一下車站，二樓有好多看起來不錯的餐廳。

Beth: You are really my brother. You have a sense of food instead of a sense of the direction.

真不虧是我哥呀，你找不到路，但是很會找餐廳呀。

Glenn: You can't blame me on that, I was so hungry that I got distracted while driving.

這能怪我嗎？我太餓了，根本不能專心開車。

Maggie: Give him a break. Let's go upstairs. I'm hungry, too.

饒了他吧，我們上樓看看，我也餓了。

Beth: Sure, whatever you said.

沒問題，你說的都好。

Maggie: So, what is your plan today, Beth?

Beth，那你今天的行程要怎麼安排呢？

Beth: Well, first, we head for Taipei 101, I want to check in at the observatory. It's going to be exciting. Then, I would like to buy some new

首先，我們去台北101，我想去觀景台打卡，一定很有趣。然後再去購物，有什麼推薦的品

outfits. Any brand that you like to recommend?

牌嗎？

Maggie: There are many famous stores near taipei101, have you ever been to forever 21? It just opened last year. Many young ladies love forever 21. They call it "fast fashion".

101 附近有許多有名的商家，你有去過 Forever 21 嗎？去年開幕的。許多年輕女生都很喜歡這個品牌，他們稱之為「快速時尚」。

 單字解析

Direction [dəˋrɛkʃən] *n.* 方向，指示
例 The nice lady showed the right direction for those tourists.
➔ 這位好心的女士幫這些觀光客指引正確的方向。

Starving [ˋstɑrvɪŋ] *adj.* 很餓的;挨餓的
例 The refugees are starving. We should do something.
➔ 難民們正在挨餓，我們應該要想想辦法。

Glance [glæns] *n.v.* 喵一眼;瞥見
例 Rick had glanced at his watched then left.
➔ Rick 看了一下他的手錶，然後就離開了。

Head [hɛd] *v.* 朝向..
例 We are heading for the park. Don't leave.

➡ 我們正朝公園走過去，不要離開。

$ 句型解析

本書生活化的對話中為您介紹實用的句型或是短句，再舉例句說明，讓您看完之後，就能馬上輕鬆學會，不用背誦！！

S+ be familiar with　熟悉

例 Jackson is very familiar with the laws. You can consult with him.

➡ Jackson 十分熟悉法律，你可以向他諮詢。

例 Kelly is not familiar with the new product, so the client got angry.

➡ Kelly 對新產品不熟，所以客戶生氣了。

So ...that　太⋯以至於

例 Micky was so happy that he started dancing.

➡ Micky 太開心了，所以他就開始跳舞。

例 The water is so dirty that no one wants to drink it.

➡ 那水太髒了，根本沒人要喝。

以上的單字及短句十分的簡單與實用，

讓您購物之餘，也能自然而然的學習英文哦。

💎 相關網站

➡ **Urban Outfitters** （圖片網址：http://www.urbanoutfitters.com）

網頁介紹：年輕時尚，又具設計感的平價服飾，十分受歡迎。

國際運送：有送台灣，經濟運送 10-12 天到，運費 USD$30。標準運送 7-10 天到，運費 USD$40.00

➡ **Juicy Couture** （圖片網址：http://www.juicycouture.com）

網頁介紹：美國女孩的甜心品牌。

國際運送：任何美國境外訂單皆轉由 Borderfree 處理。包含運送、帳單。可先結算關稅等費用。

➡ **Bebe** （圖片網址：http://www.bebe.com/）

網頁介紹：年輕時尚，帶點性感的平價服飾，十分受歡迎。

國際運送：由 International Checkout 負責運送國際。

➡ **Banana Republic** （圖片網址：http://bananarepublic.gap.com）

網頁介紹：Gap 旗下的白領年輕時尚的品牌服飾，男女裝都有。

國際運送：有國際運送，按一般購物流程選購。

➡ **Romwe** （圖片網址：http://www.romwe.com）

網頁介紹：十分平價的年輕時尚品牌服飾。

國際運送：訂單滿 USD$50 以上，享免費標準運送台灣，5-10 天到。若低於 USD$50，運費為 USD$5.99 。

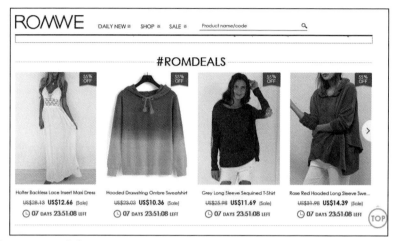

➡ **Forever 21**（圖片網址：http://www.forever21.com）

網頁介紹：美國平價女裝第一品牌。

國際運送：有運送至台灣，按一般購物流程選購。

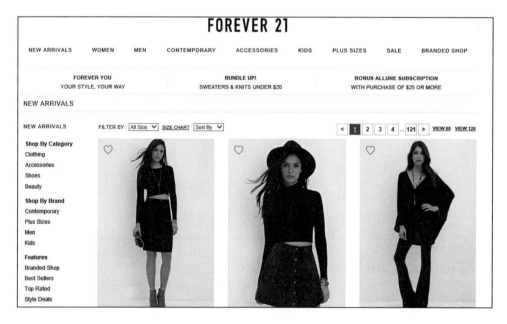

小貼士

➢ 許多美國的網站多享有美國境內免運，或是低門檻的免運。加上許多折扣也僅限於美國訂單使用。因此，可以先做比較，看自行購物運送，或是購物後由美國代運公司運送，何種划算，再決定要如何運送。

➢ 以上網站的運費資訊僅為參考，各個網站有時會出免費活動，或是更改運送規則。實際運費以您實際購物時，網站所公布的規則為準。

Word Bank

Party + Going out 聚會+外出服	Shirtdresses 長版上衣
Casual 休閒	Shift 裙裝
Rompers + Jumpsuits 連身裝 + 連身褲	Tee+Tunics 束腰上衣
Fit+ Flare 性感合身	

Unit 10
為小寶貝添新裝

◆ 童裝系列

本篇介紹的知名歐美童裝，大部分都有運送台灣。喜歡嘗新的媽媽可以試試。

◆ 情境對話

Carol: Lori, sorry I'm late. I was stuck in the traffic and the parking lot was so crowded. I had to wait in line to park my car. And the parking space is so small, I had to squeeze through there.

Lori，抱歉，我來晚了。我被困在車陣中動彈不得，而且停車場好擠，我得排隊停車。那停車位好小，很難擠進去呀。

Lori: Really?

真的嗎？

Carol: Don't look at me skeptically.

不要用懷疑的眼神看我，

I'm not exaggerating.

我沒有誇大其辭。

Lori: OK ~ I believe you. But you still buy me coffee, I have been waiting for an hour. It's really boring. <u>My phone is dead</u> and I left my power bank at home.

好吧！我相信你，但是你得買杯咖啡請我，我等了一個鐘頭，真的很無聊。我的手機沒電了，而我的行動電源放在家裡。

Carol: Well, there is an extra power bank in my bag. Let's buy the coffee and get your phone charged.

我的手提袋裡有個備用的行動電源，走！我們去買咖啡，也給你的手機充電。

Lori: Thanks, I could use that.

謝謝，我真的很需要這些。

Carol: Hey, how is everything? I haven't seen Carl for long time. How old is he?

嘿，一切都好嗎？好一陣子沒看到 Carl 了，他幾歲了？

Lori: He is 10, the 5th grade. Taller than me now.

10 歲了，上五年級，都比我高了。

Carol: Wow~Time flies. Remember once you had to leave him with me,

哇，時光飛逝。記得有一次你把他託給我照顧，他

he was crying sadly. That's really adorable.

哭得好傷心，真是很可愛。

Lori: Now, he is a big boy, it's getting harder to buy his clothes. I can't find his size in children department, and the clothes in men's department are rigid.

現在是個大男生了。而且他的衣服越來越難買，童裝部找不到他的尺寸，男裝部的衣服又太死板。

Carol: Maybe you can try online shopping. Some brands provide larger size, to 14 and 16.

或許你可以試試線上購物，有些品牌有大一點的尺碼，到 14 或 16。

單字解析

Squeeze [skwiz] *v.* 擠，壓

例 The teacher squeezed her arm hard, so there are bruises.

➜ 那個老師用力地捏她的手臂，所以有些瘀青。

Skeptically [`skɛptɪk!ɪ] *adv* 懷疑的

例 Kevin looked at the man skeptically, wondering who he was.

➜ Kevin 懷疑地看著那個男人，很好奇他是誰。

句型解析

本書生活化的對話中為您介紹實用的句型或是短句，再舉例句說明，讓您看完之後，就能馬上輕鬆學會，不用背誦！！

My phone is dead 我的手機沒電了

解 沒錯！手機沒電就是這樣說，請不要說 no electricity。

例 My phone is dead, and I have no power bank.

➡ 我手機沒電了而且我沒有行動電源。

例 Allen's phone is dead, there is no way to reach him.

➡ Allen 的手機沒電了，我們聯絡不到他了。

以上的單字及短句十分的簡單與實用，
讓您購物之餘，也能自然而然的學習英文哦。

💎 相關網站

➡ **Next** （圖片來源網址 http://tw.nextdirect.com/zh/ ）

網頁介紹：沒看錯，受歡迎的 Next 也出中文網站了，購物更便利!

國際運送：滿台幣 900，免費寄送台灣。

Part 1 教學篇

Part 2 商品篇

Part 3 旅遊篇

➡ **Janie & Jack** （圖片來源：網址 http://www.janieandjack.com）

網頁介紹：美國知名童裝品牌，男童紳士風，女童洋裝十分高雅。

國際運送：有運送台灣，採 Fedex 快遞運送，基本運費 USD$40。

⇒ **Old Navy** （圖片來源：網址 http://oldnavy.gap.com）

網頁介紹：知名平價童裝品牌。

國際運送：透過 Borderfree 運送台灣，運費因件數跟重量不同。

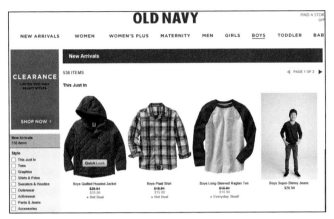

⇒ **Gymboree** （圖片來源：網址 http://www.gymboree.com）

網頁介紹：美國知名童裝品牌。

國際運送：有運送台灣，採標準，快遞運送 2 種方式。運費結帳時
會自動計算，不包含關稅等費用。

➡ **Oshkosh** （圖片來源：網址 http://www.oshkosh.com ）

網頁介紹：美國平價童裝品牌

國際運送：有運送台灣，運費因件數跟重量不同，關稅等費用預付。

➡ **Look** （圖片來源：網址 http://www.look.com ）

網頁介紹：英國平價品牌，也有童裝。

國際運送：有運送台灣，運費因件數跟重量不同。

小貼士

➤ 當您已是 Next 會員時，推薦一位朋友，且朋友有購物滿 NT1500，您則可得 NT500 的折價券，折扣代碼會由網站另外寄到您的信箱。

➤ Gymboree 首次註冊即可在下次購買時獲得額外 15%off 的折扣。

➤ 另外一家知名童裝 Carter，這家的網站直接在 Oshkosh 網站上就能看到。

➤ 以上網站的運費資訊僅為參考，各個網站有時會出免費活動，或是更改運送規則。實際運費以您實際購物時，網站所公布的規格為準。

🎩 Word Bank

Vests	背心	Sleeveless	無袖上衣
Tops and Tees	上衣	Short Sleeve	短袖上衣
Lightweight Jackets	輕量外套	Long Sleeve	長袖上衣
Hoodies	連帽上衣	Toddler	小童
Sweaters and Cardigans 毛衣 & 羊毛衣		Rompers	連身裝
Bodysuits	連身裝		

Part 1 教學篇

Part 2 商品篇

Part 3 旅遊篇

Unit 11
母嬰周邊

 母嬰用品系列

本篇介紹孕婦裝及精品嬰兒用品。

 情境對話

Lori: Thanks for the suggestion. I got some nice outfits for Carl . Price is very reasonable and design is good. Even Carl likes his new outfits. You know what he told me "Look, I'll be the coolest in my class. Girls would fall in love with me"

謝謝你的建議，我在網路上幫 Carl 買了些衣服，價格很合理，設計也很棒。重點是，連 Carl 也喜歡他的新衣服，你知道他跟我怎麼說的嗎？"看我，一定是班上最酷的，女生們都要愛上我了"。

Carol: Ha-ha, he said that? That's really amusing.

哈哈，他真的這樣說嗎？太有趣了！

Lori: Did you hear from Andrea? She called me last night.

你有跟 Andrea 聯絡嗎？她昨天打電話給我。

Carol: No ~ I thought she had moved to another city. How is she doing?

沒有，我以為她已經搬去別的城市了，她還好嗎？

Lori: She lives in Taichung now and she got married last year.

她現在住台中，去年結婚了。

Carol: Wow~ that's fast. Why didn't I get any invitation for her wedding? Did you get the invitation?

哇～這麼快，為什麼她沒有邀請我去她的婚禮呢？你有被邀請嗎？

Lori: Yes, I did, and you did too. But you were in Canada for a family trip then, remember? Last October.

有呀，你也有。但是你那時候在加拿大跟家人旅遊，去年 10 月，記得嗎？

Carol: Now you remind me.

現在你一說，我就想起來了。

Lori: She was wondering if we could get together next Wednesday. She is pregnant so her husband will come with her.

她問我們下週三能不能聚聚。因為她懷孕了，所以她先生會跟她一起來。

Carol: Her husband, Roger, right?

她先生，叫 Roger 是

Next Wednesday is fine. | 吧？下星期三我可以安排。

Lori: Me, too. I'm thinking maybe we can buy her some baby gifts. | 我也是，我在想，我們是不是該給她買個小嬰兒的禮物。

Carol: Oh ~ that's a thoughtful idea. You are right. | 哦，這真是個好主意，你說的對。

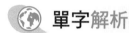 **單字**解析

Suggestion [sə`dʒɛstʃən] *n.* 建議

例 Kelly has some suggestions for the new house decoration.

➜ Kelly 對新房子的裝潢有些建議。

Reasonable [`riznəb!] *adj* 合理的

例 Their demand is not reasonable, so the mayor refuses to accept it.

➜ 他們要求很不合理，所以市長拒絕了。

Amusing [ə`mjuzɪŋ] *adj* 有趣的

例 The amusing story made the kids laugh loudly.

➜ 那個有趣的故事讓孩子們開懷大笑!

句型解析

本書生活化的對話中為您介紹實用的句型或是短句，再舉例句說明，讓您看完之後，就能馬上輕鬆學會，不用背誦！！

I thought　我以為…

解 對於過去已經發生的事情，我們可以用 I thought　我以為…來表自己的看法。

例 Why you are here？I thought you already left the office.

➡ 為什麼你還在這？我以為你已經離開辦公室了。

例 Kelly tried to abandon her dog on the street, I though that's ridiculous so I stopped her.

➡ Kelly 要在大街上遺棄她的狗，我覺得太荒謬了，所以阻止她。

以上的單字及短句十分的簡單與實用，
讓您購物之餘，也能自然而然的學習英文哦。

相關網站

➡ **Aden + Anais**

（圖片來源：網址 https://www.adenandanais.com/）

網頁介紹：美國的嬰兒用品品牌因英國皇室小王子使用而大受矚目。

國際運送：有寄送台灣，運費結帳時結算，不包含關稅等費用。

Part 1 教學篇

Part 2 商品篇

Part 3 旅遊篇

➡ **Motherhood** （圖片來源：網址 http://www.motherhood.com/）

網頁介紹：美國的知名孕婦裝品牌。

國際運送：有寄送台灣，運費結帳時結算，結算時會以台幣計價。

➡ **Swaddle Designs**

（圖片來源：網址 http://www.swaddledesigns.com/）

網頁介紹：美國的嬰兒用品品牌。

國際運送：沒有寄送台灣，可請代運公司運送。

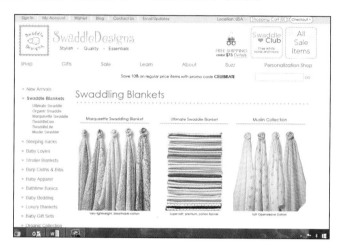

➡ **ASOS** （圖片來源:網址 http://www.asos.com）

網頁介紹：ASOS 不只有平價女裝，也有時尚孕婦裝，台幣計價。

國際運送：訂單金額滿 NT1150 享免費標準運送，14 天內到。

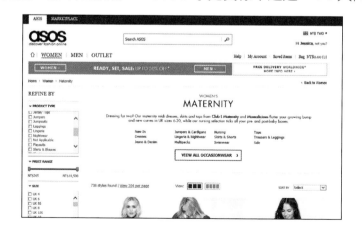

➡ **Mothercare** （圖片來源：網址 http://www.mothercare.com）

網頁介紹：英國的嬰兒用品品牌。

國際運送：有寄送台灣，運費依商品重量計價。

➡ **Marie Chantal** （圖片來源：網址 http://www.mariechantal.com）

網頁介紹：希臘王妃設計的品牌洋裝，貝克漢女兒也穿。

國際運送：有寄送台灣，運費 US$60。

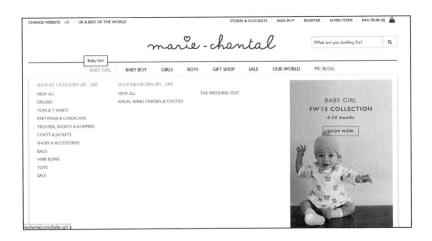

小貼士

➤ 英國的 Mothercare 商品眾多，包含孕婦 & 嬰兒用品，並也有銷售其他品牌商品。但是在選購的時候，請特別留意該項商品是否能夠運送國際。一般來說，提供國際寄送的商品僅為孕婦系列，嬰兒衣物等，像傢俱、推車等大型商品是不在運送範圍裡的。

➤ aden + Anais 雖有出售身體保養系列，但是基於國際運送法規，這類的產品無法運送。事實上，在網際購物時，要避免挑選、易碎品和液體等，或是任何在運送途中會破損的商品。這樣才能避免意外狀況出現破壞了購物的好心情

➤ 以上網站的運費資訊僅為參考，各個網站有時會出免費活動，或是更改運送規則。實際運費以您實際購物時，網站所公布的規則為準。

Word Bank

Tops	上衣	Active	休閒服
Bottoms	褲類	Nursing	哺乳衣
Dresses& Skits	洋裝&裙子	Swaddles	包巾
Lingerie	內衣	Blankets	毛毯
Sleep	睡衣	Bibs	兜巾
Outwear	外出服	Swim	泳衣

Unit **12**

內在美也很重要

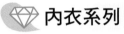 **內衣系列**

本篇要介紹一些知名的品牌內衣。

情境對話

Andrea: Carol, Lori. Over here. This restaurant is magnificent. They even have the former president pictures on the wall.

Carol，Lori。在這裡。這餐廳真不錯，他們牆上還有之前總統的照片。

Carol: Indeed, it's the famous place in the city, we made the reservation one week ago. I'm glad you like it.

的確如此，這是市裡知名的景點，我們一星期前就訂好位了，你喜歡就好。

Andrea: Thanks. You know I'm eating for two now.

我還滿喜歡的，你知道我現在都吃 2 人份的。

Carol: It's been a long time. Look at you. You are a mother. Can't wait to see your baby.

好久不見了，看看你，你要當媽媽了，真等不及看你的寶寶。

Andrea: Roger and I both are very excited. We have been expecting this baby for months. I'm sure that she will be spoiled.

我也很期待呢，Roger 跟我都很開心，我們盼望她好幾個月了，她以後一定會被寵壞的。

Lori: Speaking of Roger, where is he? I thought he is coming with you.

說到 Roger，他在哪？我以為你們要一起來的。

Andrea: Oh！he dropped me off and went to visit a friend. They want to develop a new application. Don't worry, he will pick me up later.

哦，他把我放下來之後就去跟朋友碰面了，他們要開發一個新的 APP 應用程式。別擔心，他晚點會接我。

Lori: Here, gifts from Carol and me. We hope you would like it.

這是 Carol 跟我送妳的禮物，希望你會喜歡。

Andrea: Thank you both, the soft bib and lingerie. This brand is really popular. But they don't have shop in Taiwan.

謝謝你們二位，是嬰兒圍兜跟內衣，這牌子真的很有名氣。但是它不是在台灣沒有分店嗎？

Carol: You are right. But, they have shops online and offer international shipping. It's quite convenient.

沒錯，但是他們有網路商店、線上購物跟提供全球運送，十分方便。

Andrea: I really appreciate it.

真的很謝謝你們。

Carol: <u>As long as</u> you like it, <u>it's worth it</u>.

只要你喜歡就值得了。

 單字解析

Magnificent [mæg`nɪfəsənt] *adj* 華麗的

例 The museum is a magnificent building. It attracts many tourists every year.

➡ 那博物館十分的壯觀，每年吸引許多觀光客前來。

Former [`fɔrmɚ] *adj* 以前的

例 The former mayor started to criticize the government policy

➡ 前任市長開始批評政府政策。

Reservation [ˌrɛzɚ`veʃən] *n.* 保留

例 I'm sorry, I would like to cancel our reservation.

➡ 很抱歉，我必須取消我們的訂位。

句型解析

> 本書生活化的對話中為您介紹實用的句型或是短句，再舉例句說明，讓您看完之後，就能馬上輕鬆學會，不用背誦！！

As long as　不論多久，只要

解 as long as 當字面的意思，是形容時間長短，如：

例 You can stay here as long as you like.

➡ 你可以在這裡待多久都可以。

亦可當只要，如：

例 As long as you need me, I'll be there.

➡ 只要你需要，我會一直在你身邊。

It's worth it 很值得

解 當我們想說出某事很值得時，不需要複雜單字，或是文法。只要簡單的形容詞 worth，就能形容。

例 The dinner is quite costly, but it's worth it. We can meet Buffett in person.

➡ 那晚餐雖然很昂貴但是很值得，我們能見到巴菲特本人。

> 以上的單字及短句十分的簡單與實用，
> 讓您購物之餘，也能自然而然的學習英文哦。

◆ 相關網站

➡ Victoria Secrect （圖片網址：https://www.victoriassecret.com）

網頁介紹：美國內衣知名品牌，網站以台幣計價。

國際運送：有運送台灣，運費依訂單金額而不同，結帳時計算。

➡ Bare Necessities

（圖片網址：http://www.barenecessities.com/）

網頁介紹：也是內衣知名品牌，網站以台幣計價。

國際運送：有運送台灣，運費結帳時計算。

➡ **Lane Bryant** （圖片網址：http://www.lanebryant.com）

網頁介紹：美國大尺碼內衣專賣，挑戰天使品牌。

國際運送：有運送台灣，運費結帳時計算。

➡ **Agent Provocateur**

（圖片網址：http://www.agentprovocateur.com）

網頁介紹：英國的高級內衣品牌

國際運送：有運送台灣，標準運費£10 起跳。

Part 1 教學篇

Part 2 商品篇

Part 3 旅遊篇

➡ **La Senza** （圖片網址：http://www.lasenza.com/）

網頁介紹：加拿大的著名內衣品牌，屬中價位。

國際運送：有送台灣，不論金額，運費加幣$40，採快遞運送。

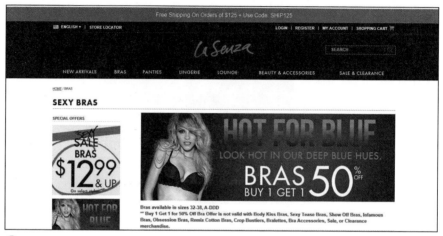

➡ **Spanx** （圖片網址：https://www.spanx.com）

網頁介紹：知名的塑身內衣品牌，網站以台幣計價。

國際運送：有送台灣，結算時計算運費。有標準運送及快遞運送。

小貼士

➤ Victoria Secret 維多莉亞的祕密多走成熟性感風，其網站旁有個 Pink 則較適合青少女，也有運動型的內衣。

➤ 除了本篇介紹的品牌之外，像是 ASOS 或是 NEXT 都有販售內衣，並享有低門檻的免運。如要選購其他商品，也可至這些網站一併購買。

➤ 以上網站的運費資訊僅為參考，各個網站有時會出免費活動，或是更改運送規則。實際運費以您實際購物時，網站所公布的規則為準。

Word Bank

Bras	內衣	DD+	大罩杯
Lingerie	內衣	Swim	泳裝
Undies	小褲	Rompers	連身衣
Panties	小褲	Jumpsuits	連身裝
Hosiery	褲襪	Sleepwear	睡衣
Accessories	配件	Fragrance	香水

Part 1 教學篇

Part 2 商品篇

Part 3 旅遊篇

Part 3

旅遊篇

Unit 1
機票哪裡找

 網頁註冊篇

自助旅行第一步，就是要先查詢機票。本篇要介紹常用的機票網站，

情境對話

Rick: The summer vacation is approaching, we should arrange family trip with the kid. How do you think?

就快要放暑假了，我們應該準備安排個家庭旅遊跟孩子一起出遊。妳覺得如何？

Meredith: That's a good idea. Carl is **big enough** to travel with us. Maybe we should ask his opinion. Carl, Daddy is taking you for vacation. Where do you want to go?

這主意不錯，Carl 已經長大了可以跟我們一起去旅行。或許我們該問問他的意見。Carl，爸爸說想帶你出去玩，你想去哪裡？

Carl: Legoland!

樂高樂園。

Meredith: Legoland? I heard there is a Legoland in Malaysia.

樂高樂園？聽説馬來西亞有個樂高樂園。

Rick: And Denmark, too.

丹麥也有！

Meredith: What? That's in Europe, it's far away. I'm not sure if he can behave well on the plane over 10 hours. Kids are unpredictable.

什麼？丹麥在歐洲，太遠了。我不認為 Carl 能乖乖在飛機上待 10 個小時。

Rick: Don't worry. They have video game on the plane. Believe me, he will be fine. Besides, we had never been to Europe, and the Euro currency rate is pretty good now. **What would you say** ?

別擔心，飛機上有電子遊樂設施，相信我，他會好的很。而且，我們沒去過歐洲，歐元匯率目前不錯。妳覺得呢？

Meredith: Well, That's a big plan. I don't know if there is a direct flight from Taipei to Copenhagen. Maybe we need to transfer in Amsterdam. And I heard the Legoland is in Billund, not Copenhagen.

這真是的大計畫，我不確定台北有飛機直達哥本哈根。或許我們得在阿姆斯特丹轉機，而且，聽説樂高樂園是在 Billund，不是哥本哈根。

Rick: Let me see, yes. You are right. The Legoland is in Billund, it takes 3 hours train from Copenhagen to Billund. We can manage it.

我來查查。沒錯！樂高樂園在 Billund，從哥本哈根坐火車 3 個小時就到了。我們能夠處理這事的。

 單字解析

transfer [træns`fɚ] *v.* 轉機，轉學，匯款

例 Jose just transferred some money to the client.

➡ Jose 剛匯款給那位客人。

manage [`mænɪdʒ] *v.* 處理

例 We will manage the problem. Don't worry.

➡ 我們會設法解決這問題，別擔心。

 句型解析

本書生活化的對話中為您介紹實用的句型或是短句，再舉例句說明，讓您看完之後，就能馬上輕鬆學會，不用背誦！！

adj + enough 足夠……

解 enough 足夠是個很實用的單字，可以搭配幾個簡單的形容詞，就能靈活運用。請看例句說明。

例 The house is big enough.There are only 3 of us.

➡ 這房子夠大了，我們只有 3 個人。

例 Jose is tall enough to reach the rack.

➡ Jose 夠高可以碰到那個架子。

What would you say? 你說呢？

解 當我們表達出自己的意見之後，想聽聽對方的說法，或是帶有爭取對方認同，邀請對方加入的意味。

例 A: We are going to have a picnic this weekend, what would you say?

B: Sure ! We would like to join you.

➡ A：我們週末要去野餐，你覺得如何？

B：當然，我們願意跟你們一起去。

以上的單字及短句十分的簡單與實用，
讓您規劃行程之餘，也能自然而然的學習英文哦。

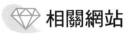 **相關網站**

➡ **Travel Star 燦星旅遊**

（圖片來源網址：http://www.startravel.com.tw）

➢ 以台北 TPE 來回哥本哈根 CPH 為例，輸入搜索條件可得。

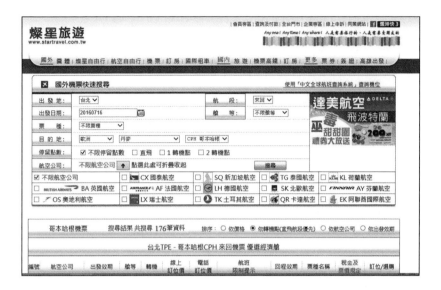

➡ **Ez Travel 易遊網** （圖片來源網址：http://www.eztravel.com.tw）

➢ 以台北 TPE 來回哥本哈根 CPH 為例，輸入搜索條件可得。

➡ **China Airlines 中華航空**

（圖片來源網址：http://www.china-airlines.com/ch/index.html）

➢ 以台北 TPE 來回香港 HKG 為例，輸入搜索條件可得機票。

➡ **China Airlines 中華航空精緻旅遊**

（圖片來源網址：http://dp.china-airlines.com/PRO/index）

➢ 華航推出的機 + 酒行程，網站上有各景點資訊，十分豐富。

➡ **EVA AIR 長榮航空**

（圖片來源網址：http://www.evaair.com/zh-tw/index.html）

➢ 以台北 TPE 來回休士頓 IAH 為例，輸入搜索條件可得機票。

Part
1
教學篇

Part
2
商品篇

Part
3
旅遊篇

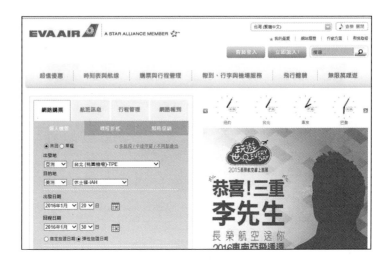

➡ **169travel** （圖片來源網址：http://www.169travel.com/）

> 強大的機票網站，可不同點進出，航段選擇等。

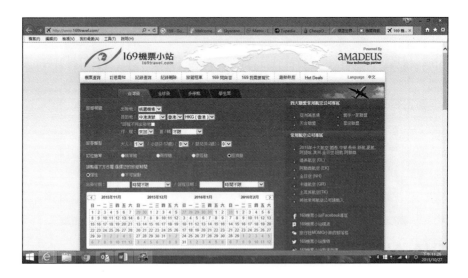

💟 小貼士

> 如果您的行程十分簡單，沒有轉機點，同一點進出，如，華航飛大阪

來回。這時除了比價網站之外，亦可上各航空公司的官網查看。有時候各航空公司會針對自家會員推出里程折抵機票，或是會員卡有額外折扣等。

➤ 搜尋機票的時候，一定要注意機場稅及燃油附加費，單看機票票價是絕對不夠的。因為機場稅及燃油附加費每家不相同，有的機票乍看之下好像十分優惠，但是其機場稅及燃油附加費卻是高得嚇人。

➤ 每個國際機場都有其機場代碼，譬如說桃園機場為 TPE，日本成田機場為 NAA，香港為 HKG。可以先上網搜尋機場代碼，這樣能更快的查到您要的機票。

➤ 訂位成功之後，會得到一組公司訂位代號。短程的航程，如台北-香港。若我們想要臨時更改行程，改變航班，可以打電話給航空公司客服，提供此代號即可處理。但是長程航程，或是聯航（包含 2 家航空公司以上），要更改行程就不是這麼容易的事。所以長程旅程的行程在規劃時，需更加謹慎。

🎩 Word Bank

Round Trip	來回票	Outbound Date	出發日期
One-way	單程	Return Date	回程日期
Multi-City	不同點進出	Cabin	艙等
Destination	目的地	Currency	幣別

💎 情境對話

Meredith: Hi, April, I didn't know you live nearby.

嗨，April，我不知道你住這附近。

April: Meredith, what a coincidence! Actually, I'm on my way home, just stop to buy some grocery.

Meredith，好巧呀。事實上，我正在要回家的路上，剛停下來買點東西。

Meredith: It's pretty late, worked over time?

很晚了，你加班嗎？

April: No, my car got a flat tire, and I had waited for tire replacement. It took 2 hours. Hey, I heard some news, while I was in the office.

沒有，我的車胎爆了，等換胎花了 2 個鐘頭。但是我在辦公室時有聽到點消息。

Meredith: What's news? Don't be so sneaking.

什麼消息？不要神秘兮兮的。

April: Well, the general manager will appoint you as new sales manager next month. <u>It's settled</u>, and they will <u>make it official</u> soon.

總經理下個月要指派你為業務經理，已經確定了，他們很快就會正式公布這消息了。

Meredith: Wow~ I'm surprised. Who told you?

哇，受寵若驚。誰跟你說的？

April: Well, I overheard the conversation between Christina and general manger this afternoon.

我今天下午碰巧聽到 Christina 跟總經理的對話。

Meredith: Well, then, that's quite possible.

那麼，這樣的話，這消息就可能是真的。

April: Hey, that's a good news, right?

嘿，這是個好消息，是吧？

Meredith: I'm delighted with the promotion, but it means more responsibility as well. Under the economic depression, it's not easy to increase

我很高興能夠得到升遷，但是升遷也代表要承擔更多的責任。現在經濟不景氣，要增加我們的銷售規

Part
1
教學篇

Part
2
商品篇

Part
3
旅遊篇

our sales scale now.

模實在不容易。

April: Don't worry, you got me. I'm your special 3D drawing expert.

別擔心，你有我呢。我是本部門的專業 3D 繪圖者。

Meredith: Thanks for the support. Maybe I should take a short break before the official announcement. I always want to go to Copenhagen. I heard it's a beautiful city.

多謝你支持。或許我該在正式的升職通知下來前，先休個假。我一直很想去哥本哈根。聽說那是很美麗的城市。

April: That's a brilliant idea.

這主意不錯。

單字解析

Coincidence [ko`ɪnsɪdəns] *n.* 巧合

例 It's such a coincidence that they met in Taipei.

➔ 他們能在台北碰面真是太巧了。

Announcement [ə`naʊnsmənt] *n.* 聲明

例 The mayor made an announcement to respond the scandal.

➔ 市長針對那個醜聞發表聲明。

句型解析

本書生活化的對話中為您介紹實用的句型或是短句,再舉例
句說明,讓您看完之後,就能馬上輕鬆學會,不用背誦!!

It's settled 都安排好了

解 settle 動詞。有解決、安頓之意。Settled 過去分詞表示都已經解
決,處理好了。十分實用的短句。

例 A: Are we driving to airport tomorrow?

B: Don't worry. It's settled, a taxi will pick us up.

➔ A: 我們明天開車去機場嗎?

B: 別擔心,都安排好了,有計程車會來接我們。

Make it official 正式宣布

解 official 正式的,官方的。Make it official 就是將某件未定之事,正
式化,公開聲明的意思。

例 Obviously, Kelly is a qualified leader. She leads the team
efficiently. We should make it official.

➔ 很明顯的,Kelly 是個合格的領導者。她有效地領導整個團隊,我們
應該正式宣布這件事。

以上的單字及短句十分的簡單與實用,

讓您規劃行程之餘,也能自然而然的學習英文哦。

Part 1 教學篇

Part 2 商品篇

Part 3 旅遊篇

相關網站

➡ **Travel Star** 燦星旅遊

（圖片來源網址：http://www.startravel.com.tw）

➤ 舉例 搜尋日本北海道、札幌的飯店。

➡ **EZ Travel** 易遊網 （圖片來源網址：http://hotel.eztravel.com.tw）

➤ 舉例：搜尋美國西雅圖的飯店。

➡ **EZfly** 易飛網 （圖片來源網址？http://www.ezfly.com）

➤ 舉例：搜尋法國巴黎的飯店。

➡ **booking.com**（圖片來源網址：http://www.booking.com）

➢ 舉例 搜尋日本大阪帝國飯店。

➡ **tripadvisor**（圖片來源網址：http://www.tripadvisor.com.tw/）

➢ 舉例：搜尋泰國、曼谷的飯店。

Part
1
教學篇

Part
2
商品篇

Part
3
旅遊篇

➡ **Hotels.com** （圖片來源網址：http://tw.hotels.com/）

> ➢ 舉例 搜尋丹麥哥本哈根的飯店。

💟 小貼士

> ➢ 選飯店的過程，除了各大飯店網站比較之外，也不要忘記到該飯店的
> 官方網站查看。有時候，飯店官網也會推出一些不錯的專案，或是加

入會員享受連住升等的優惠。

➤ 每個人選擇飯店的標準不一樣，以年輕旅客來說，飯店價格經濟為考量重點。若是家庭旅遊，又有小朋友需要手推車的，就以近地鐵站等交通因素為考量重點。**不論您的需求為何，最重要的要顧及安全性。**飯店位置不要在太過偏僻、太複雜的地區，或出入分子不單純，這些請盡量避免。

➤ 飯店官網上秀出最好最大的房間，通常跟我們一般住的標準間，商務套房是不太一樣的。國外的旅遊網站如 Booking、Tripadvisor 還提供了住過的旅客的經驗分享，還有住過的旅客所拍攝的實際照片給您參考。

🧢 Word Bank

Hotel Guide	飯店介紹	Accommodation	住宿
Restaurant & Bar 餐廳 & 酒吧		Meeting & Banquet 宴會 & 會議	
Sports & Fitness 運動 & 健身		Sightseeing	觀光
Access	交通路線	Reservation	預約
Check in	入住	Check out	退房
Guest	旅客		

Part 1 教學篇

Part 2 商品篇

Part 3 旅遊篇

自由行的行程，有時候我們會比較晚進飯店 check in，或是帶著小朋友想要詢問飯店有沒有提供其他額外服務等。本篇要告訴您如何先去信跟飯店聯絡。

💎 情境對話

April: How is your travel plan? Have you bought the ticket yet?

旅遊計畫的如何？ 機票買好了嗎？

Meredith: No, I haven't decided it yet. There are so many choices. Copenhagen is very attractive to me. But Amsterdam is as well. You know there is a Van Gosh museum in Amsterdam.

我還不確定，有好多選擇。哥本哈根很吸引我，但是阿姆斯特丹也不錯。你知道阿姆斯特丹有個梵谷的博物館。

April: I didn't know you are a big fan of Van Gosh.

我不知道你是個藝術迷，喜歡梵谷。

Meredith: My favorite is "Starry Night". I like the mysterious blue in that painting. It's so fascinating.

我最喜歡的是「星夜」這幅畫。那神秘的藍色好美，令人著迷。

April: I know that painting, it's the fame of Van Gosh. But, I thought MOMA has it, not the Van Gosh museum.

我知道那幅畫，是梵谷的代表作。但是我想那副畫應該在 MOMA，不在梵谷博物館。

Meredith: MOMA ? What's that ?

MOMA？那是什麼？

April: Museum of Modern Art in New York.

紐約現代藝術博物館。

Meredith: Are you seriously? I didn't know that.

真的嗎？我怎麼不知道。

April: My cousin went to New York last summer break. She also visited MOMA and sent me a post card. You can check it online right now.

我表妹去年春假的時候去了紐約一趟，也去了現代藝術博物館還寄明信片給我。你可以現在上網查看看。

Meredith: You are right. Thanks for the information. Otherwise, I will

你說對了，謝謝你告訴我這資訊。不然我就糗了，

Part 1 教學篇

Part 2 商品篇

Part 3 旅遊篇

make an embarrassing mistake. Now I have to change my plan. Without " Starry Night", I prefer to go to Copenhagen.

現在計畫要重排了。沒有「星夜」的話，我比較想去哥本哈根。

April: They said the best latte is in Copenhagen. <u>You won't regret it.</u>

聽説哥本哈根的拿鐵咖啡很有名。你不會後悔的。

 ## 單字解析

Museum KK[mjuˋzɪəm] *n.* 博物館

例 The museum is closed today, we should check the information in advance,

➡ 那博物館今天沒有開放，我們應該事先查好資料的。

 ## 句型解析

本書生活化的對話中為您介紹實用的句型或是短句，再舉例句說明，讓您看完之後，就能馬上輕鬆學會，不用背誦！！

You won't regret it. 你不會後悔的

解 説出這句話，通常是給自己的話掛保證。

例 Our apples are very juicy. You won't regret it.

➡ 我們的蘋果香甜多汁，不會讓你後悔的。

例 The Japanese ryokan is very famous。You won't regret it.

➡ 這家日式溫泉飯店十分有名，不會讓你失望的。

以上的單字及短句十分的簡單與實用，

讓您規劃行程之餘，也能自然而然的學習英文哦。

 相關網站

➡ 通知飯店較晚抵達

（圖片來源：http://www.operahotelcopenhagen.com/）

➤ 在飯店的官網，通常會有聯絡資訊 Contact US 找到電子郵件就可以
直接去信飯店，聯絡詢問大小事項。

Part
1
教學篇

Part
2
商品篇

Part
3
旅遊篇

Dear Sir

I booked in your hotel, the reversation information is

Date : April 9th to April 12th. (3 nights)

Guests name: Hello Kitty

Due to the travel plan, I will arrive Copenhagen very late. The estimated time to your hotel will be around 10PM April 9th.

This is a late check-in notice, pls keep my reservation.

Thank you.

> 為保險起見,若太晚抵達飯店,可事先去信通知飯店。提供入住日期、旅客姓名、預計到達的時間。飯店人員收到您的來信之後,會再回信給您,收到確認之後,就可更安心的出遊。

➡ **詢問飯店是否可提供小嬰兒床**

（圖片來源網址 http://www.thearthotel.com/contact-us.html）

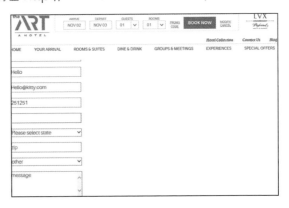

有些飯店網頁是提供表格給您填寫。

> Dear Sir
>
> We had booked your hotel, our stay will be
>
> Date: 20th May-23th May
> Guests name: Jason Ho, Lisa Ho.
> Room: Standard
>
> Our baby will also travel with us. We would like to know if you could add an extra baby bed in the room. Thank you.

　　帶小寶寶旅行有些特殊需求，如加嬰兒小床，有無嬰兒澡盆等。您可以去信先詢問飯店人員，若有的話可請飯店先準備好。

➡ 詢問飯店附近是否有租車公司

圖片來源網址 https://www.keioplaza-sapporo.co.jp

> Dear Sir.
>
> We booked your hotel from 10th July-15th July.
>
> Guest Name: Marvin and Winnie Chung.
>
> We would like to know if there is any car rental company near your hotel.
>
> Thank you.

通常跟飯店聯絡時，若已完成訂房，請提供飯店您的訂房資料。如此飯店人員才能更迅速、正確的回覆給您。

 小貼士

➤ 寫英文信的小技巧，簡單即可，不用生澀的單字。重點是讓雙方的意思清楚地表達出來。您可以參考本篇的三邊短文，再將您的需求置換即可。

➤ 我們國人最喜歡的旅遊點日本，因為匯率的關係又更顯熱門。許多人喜歡到日本購物，甚至會先在日本網站上購買好，寄到住宿的旅館。若您真的必須先寄東西到飯店，請先去信通知飯店，告知商品預定到的時間、件數。最好是在您下榻的時候，商品才寄到。件數也應越少越好，越輕越好，避免給飯店帶來困擾。

🎩 **Word Bank**

Standard room	標準房	Executive room	行政套房
Superior room	高級房	Special offer	特別專案
Contact us	與我們聯繫		

💎 情境對話

Christina: Meredith, I heard that you will take few days off next week.

Meredith，聽說你下週要請假幾天。

Meredith: Yes, I'm planning to Europe with my family for 2 weeks.

對的。我計畫跟家人去歐洲 2 星期。

Christina: That's wonderful. Where do you go ? Paris ?

好棒，你們要去哪裡？巴黎嗎？

Meredith: Are you kidding? When travelling with kids, the romantic place is not the optional. We are going to Denmark and Sweden to visit the museum and Legoland.

別開玩笑了，帶著小孩怎能去那些浪漫的地方。我們要去丹麥跟瑞典,去逛逛博物館跟樂高樂園。

Christina: That sounds a great trip. You know there are many famous modern design craft in Denmark, even Pandora is from Denmark.

聽起來很不錯呀。你知道嗎，丹麥有許多知名的現代設計工藝品，連 Pandora 也是丹麥的。

April: Pandora? <u>You mean</u> the jewelry, Pandora?

Pandora？你是說珠寶的 Pandora？

Christina: I guess so. As far as I know, there is only Pandora from Denmark.

我猜是吧。就我所知，丹麥就一個 Pandora。

April: Meredith, you should get yourself the Pandora charms. It's so popular now. You can create your own style, exclusive charm. Look, I got one.

Meredith，你該給你自己做條 Pandora 手鍊，你可以自己設計自我風格，獨一無二的手鍊。最近大受歡迎。你看，我也有一條。

Meredith: That's beautiful. You always follow the trends. Thanks for the information. I'll check that when I'm in Copenhagen.

很漂亮的手鍊，你總是跟得上流行趨勢。謝謝您的建議。我到哥本哈根的時候會去看看的。

Christina: Hey, have you gotten the

嘿，你拿到正式的升職通

official promotion announcement yet？　知了嗎？

Meredith: Not yet, but the general manager already informed me <u>in person</u>. And he also approved of my Europe trip. So, I can have a long vacation before the official announcement.

還沒有，但是總經理已經當面告知我了，我要請假的事他也准了。所以在正式的通知下來之前，我能好好的休假。

 ## 單字解析

Romantic [rə`mæntɪk] *adj/n.* 浪漫的
例 They had romantic dinner together and decided to get married.
➜ 他們共享一頓浪漫的晚餐並決定要結婚了。

Optional [`ɑpʃən!] *adj* 可選擇的
例 The field trip is optional. You can decide it by yourself.
➜ 戶外教學沒有強制性，你可以自行決定要不要去。

句型解析

 本書生活化的對話中為您介紹實用的句型或是短句，再舉例句說明，讓您看完之後，就能馬上輕鬆學會，不用背誦!!

You mean 你的意思是說……

解 十分口語的一句話，我們還可以將主詞換掉，做變化。請看例句。

例 A: Sorry, I just got a phone call from my company. It's kind of urgent.

B: You mean you are not going with us?

➜ A: 抱歉，我剛接到公司電話，有些急事。

B: 你是說你不跟我們去了？

例 The latest design is very creative. I mean people will like it, right?

➜ 最新的設計十分的有創意。我的意思是說，人們會喜歡這設計，對吧？

in person 親自，當面

例 Sandra would like to give this gift to her uncle in person.

➜ Sandra 想要當面將這禮物交給她舅舅。

以上的單字及短句十分的簡單與實用，讓您規劃行程之餘，也能自然而然的學習英文哦。

 **相關網站**

➡ 舉例 從哥本哈根 **Copenhagen** 車站到 **Billund** 的樂高樂園

（圖片來源網址：http://www.dsb.dk/om-dsb/in-english/）

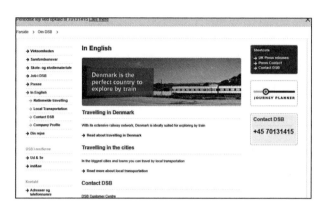

Step1. 到搜尋網站找，Denmark train，到丹麥國鐵網站 DSB
Step2. 點入右手邊的 Journey Planner 旅程計畫。

➡ 輸入出發點及目的地。

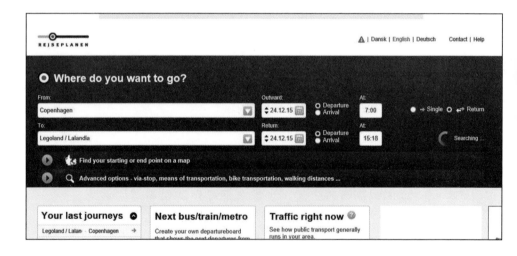

From：選擇我們的起點 Copenhagen　　　Outward：去程日
To:　　選擇目的地　　Legoland　　　　Return：回程日
Departure 及 Arrival，我們可以填入出發的時間，或是到達的時間。
Single：表示單程；Return：為來回旅程。

➡ 選擇行程

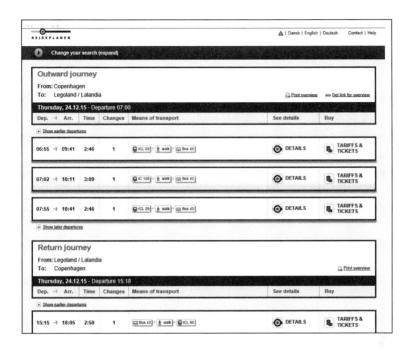

行程輸入之後，網站會根據我們的條件列出適合行程。

Outward Journey 出發行程，共有 3 個行程可以選擇。

➢ 圖表說明:

6:55 出發- 09:41 到 航程 2:46 分。坐火車 ICL25，轉 43 號公車

7:02 出發- 10:11 到 航程 3:09 分。坐火車 IC125，轉 43 號公車

7:55 出發- 10:41 到 航程 2:46 分。坐火車 ICL29，轉 43 號公車

回程亦同：會列出符合我們輸入時間點的行程，讓我們選擇。

⇒ 行程細節

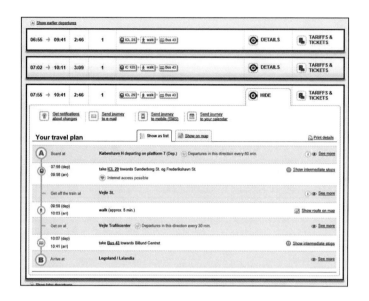

　　DSB 旅遊資訊十分詳盡，有清單説明（show as list），地圖説明（show on map）

➤ 您可以再點入 Details 詳情，來查看旅程的細節。説明如下：

　　07:55 從哥本哈根的 7 號月台 出發的 ICL29 車上有網路

　　09:58 到達，在 Vejle St 下車。

　　走 5 分鐘到 Vejle Trafikcenter 乘坐 43 號公車。

　　10:07 發車　10:41 到達 Legoland.

➤ 若您還不清楚的話，點選 see more 看更多，有街景圖。

➤ 旁邊的圖示，火車，行人，公車，表示使用的交通工具。

➤ 購票程序請見下一篇

小貼士

➤ 在剛接觸到國外火車網站時，網站上大量的資訊跟全英文的介面，往往會讓旅客不知道如何下手，這是很正常的現象。只要多花點時間看懂網站操作方法、訂票的流程，細心地確認各個細節，慢慢就能上手。

➤ 出國旅遊時，要將您在網路上購買的機票，車票的信用卡都必須隨身攜帶。有時候航空櫃台，或站務人員要查看此信用卡。

Word Bank

Travel	旅行	Outward	去程
Return	回程	Departure	出發
Arrival	抵達	Details	細節
Ticket	票務	Platform	月台
Get notification about the changes 若行程異動，請通知		Send journey to e-mail 將行程寄到信箱	

Part
1
教學篇

Part
2
商品篇

Part
3
旅遊篇

輕鬆搞定二地交通（下）

💎 情境對話

Christina: Meredith, do you have a minute? I just got an e-mail from T&J tooling. Mr. Grey is coming next week.

Meredith，有空嗎？我剛收到 T&J tooling 工具的來信。Grey 先生下週要來訪。

Meredith: What's the main purpose of his trip ?

他此行的目的為何？

Christina: For the shipping inspection. Last shipment, there were some damaged cartons in the container and **resulted in** claim.

他要檢查裝船驗貨。上批出貨中，貨櫃裡有幾個紙箱損壞，結果被客訴了。

Meredith: I remember that claim. It's costly. Mr. Grey is very strict with ev-

我記得那個客訴，花了好多錢。Grey 先生對細節

ery detail. But I won't be in the office next week. We should come up with a corresponding strategy this afternoon.

Christina: I just informed our factory, Alex, the head of the quality control departmet, will participate in our meeting.

Meredith: Well done. You can read my mind in advance.

Alex: After checking with all relative workers, we found the reason of damaged carton was weather. Those packing cartons stocked outside. We already discarded the remaining cartons, all brand new cartons stock inside the warehouse now.

Meredith: That's ridiculous mistake, Because of the weather? You mean we could avoid this problem before?

要求的十分嚴格。可是下週我不在辦公司，下午我們應該開會來討論應對的方案。

我剛才通知工廠了，Alex，品管部門的主管也會來參加我們的會議。

安排得很好，你能預知我的想法。

經過跟所有相關人員確認之後，我們找到了箱子損壞的原因，是因為天氣。包裝箱一直都放在戶外。我們已經將剩下的箱子丟棄，全新的包裝箱目前都放在倉庫裡。

因為天氣的關係？這真是個荒謬的錯誤。你的意思是說我們之前本來可以避免這問題的嗎？

Christina: Do you have any idea how much trouble this mistake caused? The customer had filed the claim last month.

你知道這個失誤引起多大問題嗎？ 客戶上個月提出客訴了。

Alex: That's my responsibility. I wouldn't dodge it. But I guarantee that it won't happen again.

這是我應該承擔的責任，我不會閃躲。但是我可以確保，這個問題不會再發生第二次了。

Meredith: Let's hope so.

希望如此。

 ## 單字解析

Purpose [`pɝ·pəs] *n./v.* 目的

例 The purpose of this occasion is to bring us together.

➤ 這次聚會的目的是大家可以聚一聚。

Damage [`dæmɪdʒ] *n./v.* 損壞

例 Bring the umbrella, or the sun can damage your skin.

➤ 帶著洋傘吧，否則太陽對你的皮膚不好。

Corresponding [ˌkɔrɪ`spɑndɪŋ] *adj.* 對應的

例 The wallpaper color is not corresponding to the contract, there must be some mistakes.

➜　這壁紙的顏色跟合約不一樣，一定有什麼地方出錯了。

 句型解析

本書生活化的對話中為您介紹實用的句型或是短句，再舉例句說明，讓您看完之後，就能馬上輕鬆學會，不用背誦 !!

Resulted in 引起，導致

解 result 結果，result in 則為引起、導致之意。記得將引起的原因放在前面，產生的結果放在後面。

例 The hurricane resulted in a serious flood.

➜　颶風引起洪水。

例 Their meeting had resulted in many problems.

➜　他們的會面引起了許多的問題

以上的單字及短句十分的簡單與實用，
讓您規劃行程之餘，也能自然而然的學習英文哦。

相關網站

➜ 舉例 從哥本哈根 **Copenhagen** 車站要到 **Billund** 的樂高樂
園 （圖片來源網址：http://www.dsb.dk/om-dsb/in-english/）

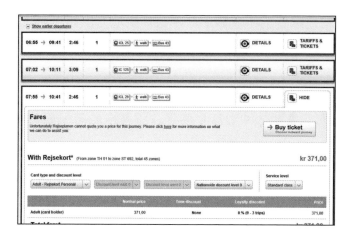

行程細節看完之後，選取您要的來回行程。進入購票 Buy ticket。

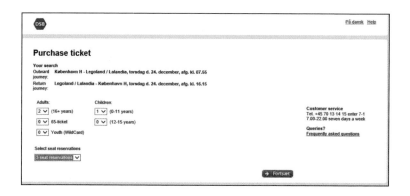

➡ 購買車票 Purchase ticket.

下方是我們選的來回行程，請再核對一次。

輸入 Adult 成人-人數，Children 兒童-人數

Select sear reservations 預選位。

➢ 選位是要加價的

➢ 這裡支付的票價是火車票價，公車的車票是上車支付的，沒有預售

➡ 票價細節

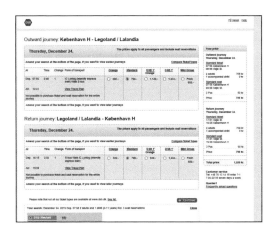

2 大 1 小的來回票火車票，另外加上預選座位的費用。

每個細節都要再三確認，來回行程重看一次。

➡ 預選座位

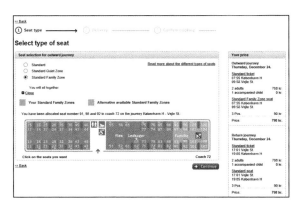

Select seat type 選擇座位種類。

Standard family zone 標準家庭區

➡ 自行列印車票

> Delivery 寄送有 2 個選項- Print at home 在家列印、Collect 取票。選擇在家列印者，需提供電子信箱。付款完成之後，就會收到電子車票，請自行印出。（需有 Adobe 程式）

> 提供核對身分的信用卡 Presentation of ID on the train. 填入旅客之一的信用卡資料，此張信用卡必須隨身攜帶，以供檢查。

➡ 確認付款

小貼士

➢ 丹麥是個十分有秩序的國家，乘坐火車、地鐵時，不論進站、出站都沒有閘門驗票，由旅客自由進出。政府相信，旅客會自動自發地購買車票再乘車。然而，一旦逃票被抓到，就必須面臨高額的罰款。所以千萬不要嘗試任何非法的行為。

➢ 在台灣使用信用卡時，並不會使用到 pin code。但是，在國外使用信用卡時，有時候售票機會要求我們輸入 pin code。所以在出國之前，先致電信用卡客服，跟銀行索取 pin code，銀行會將此密碼函寄給您，是一組 4 位數的密碼。

Word Bank

Adult	成人	Children	兒童
Normal Price	一般價格	Purchase ticket	購票
Select seat reservation 選位		Standard seat 標準座	
Standard Quiet Zon 標準安靜座		Standard Family Zone 標準家庭座	
Print at home	在家列印	Total Price	總價

Part 1 教學篇

Part 2 商品篇

Part 3 旅遊篇

Unit **6**
歐洲跨國火車

 情境對話

Christina: I can't believe that the claim was caused by an insignificant reason.

我不敢相信客訴居然是這麼微不足道的理由所引起的。

Alex: <u>In specific</u>, 2 months ago, we were replacing the facility. To make more space, some package cartons were moved outside. Just 2 days, those cartons were slightly wet and no one noticed it.

詳細地來說，2 個月前廠裡正在更換設備，為了空出更多空間。我們將一些紙箱搬出倉庫，才 2 天的時間這些紙箱就稍微受潮了，而且沒有人注意到。

Christina: If so, there should be more claim. However, So far, T& J tooling is the only customer who filed

如果是像你説的，應該有更多客訴才是。但是目前只有 T & J tooling 這

the claim.

客戶提出客訴。

Alex: Those cartons were customized for T& J. only.

這些紙箱是特別訂做給 T&J 使用的。

Christina: Ok, finally we figure out the cause of claim. We should have the official report and submit it to the General manager, then we can avoid the same problem next time. That's the purpose of our meeting.

好，我們終於找出客訴的原因了。我們必須寫份正式的報告上交給總經理。這樣下次我們才能避免相同的問題。這才是會議的主要目的。

Meredith: <u>I can't agree with you anymore</u>.

我十分同意你的説法。

Christina: Should we notify Mr. Grey about the meeting result?

你認為我們應該讓 Mr. Grey 知道這些原因嗎？

Meredith: Well, honesty is the best policy. We figured out the cause, and take the responsibility of damaged cartons.

誠實為上，我們找出原因了，也賠償那些損壞的箱子了。

Christina: Ok, I'll explain to Mr. Grey when he is visiting. There shouldn't

好，當 Mr.Grey 來訪時，我會跟他們解釋清

Part 1 教學篇

Part 2 商品篇

Part 3 旅遊篇

be any problem. Don't worry. April and I can handle this.

楚。應該沒有問題的，別擔心。April 跟我會將這事好好處理的。

Meredith: I know that I can count on you.. Besides, the fact is I already booked the air ticket and Europe train ticket. It's too late to cancel all those schedule.

我知道你很可靠。謝謝，事實上，我飛機票跟火車票都買好了，要取消行程實在太遲了。

單字解析

Insignificant [ˌɪnsɪgˈnɪfəkənt] *adj* 微小的

例 Those insignificant information is not helpful, so we should try another method.

➡ 這些不重要的資訊對我們沒有幫助，所以我們得想別的辦法。

Facility [fəˈsɪlətɪ] *n.* 設備

例 The advanced facility can lead us to the future.

➡ 先進的設備能夠帶領我們走向未來。

Slightly [ˈslaɪtlɪ] *adv.* 輕微的

例 Each student studies in a slightly different way.

➡ 每個學生的學習方法各有些差異。

Customize [ˋkʌstəmˌaɪz] *v.* 訂做

例 Lori looks great in the customized dress.

➤ Lori 穿著那訂做的洋裝看起來很美。

Notify [ˋnotəˌfaɪ] *v.* 通知

例 Claire was notified that her car was stolen .

➤ Claire 收到通知，表示她的車失竊了。

Responsibility [rɪˌspɑnsəˋbɪlətɪ] *n.* 責任

例 No one is willing to take the responsibility of the accident.

➤ 沒有人願意為這個意外負責。

 句型解析

本書生活化的對話中為您介紹實用的句型或是短句，再舉例句說明，讓您看完之後，就能馬上輕鬆學會，不用背誦 !!

In specific 具體的，特定的

例 Aaron's life is very mysterious. He never talked about his work in specific

➤ Aaron 的生活很神祕，他對他的工作絕口不提。

例 The dengue fever was detected in specific areas.

➤ 在一些特定地區偵測到登革熱。

Part 1 教學篇

Part 2 商品篇

Part 3 旅遊篇

I can't agree with you anymore 我非常同意

解 單看字面的解釋是我不能同意你更多了。轉換成通順的中文則是我非常同意你。

例 A: The insurance company is not reliable at all. They just want your money.

B: I can't agree with you anymore.

➡ A: 那保險公司真不可靠,他們只想要你的錢而已。

B: 我非常同意你的説法。

以上的單字及短句十分的簡單與實用,
讓您規劃行程之餘,也能自然而然的學習英文哦。

◈ 相關網站

➡ **從丹麥哥本哈根乘坐火車至瑞典斯德哥爾摩**

(圖片來源網址:https://www.sj.se/?l=en 瑞典國鐵)

➢ Step1. 在蒐尋網站上,鍵入 Sweden Train 即會出現網站。

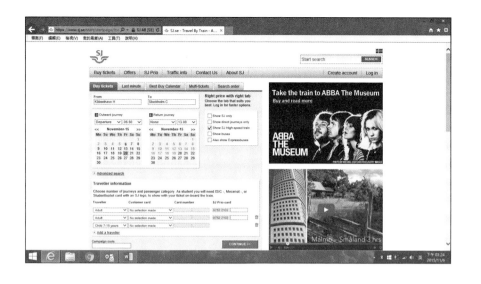

> Step2. 填入要搭乘的區段資料，旅客人數等

在購買 buy ticket 欄位中填入 From 出發地及 To 目的地，Departure 出發時間。

需初步填入旅客資料 Traveller information.

依人數填寫，2 位成人，1 位兒童，兒童須註記年齡。

> Step3.得到時刻表&票價表

瑞典國鐵車票分為：一等車廂 1st class，二等車廂 2nd class

車票也分為:3 種價格。

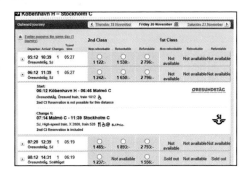

> Step4：選定要乘坐的列車

點選進去，可看到詳細資料，包含轉乘。

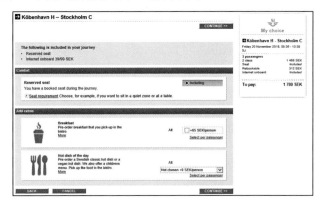

> Step5：可以加選車上餐點，右上角有票價資訊。

有早餐，及一般餐點可以選擇。可以先預選好。

若是沒有先購買餐點，臨時也可至餐車車廂去購買。

> Step6: 確認行程。

　　要刷卡之前，網站會再跟您確認一次。請詳細核對資料，若是車票是不可退換的。一旦買錯了，是沒有退款的哦。

 ## 小貼士

> 以本篇舉列的瑞典來說，車票價格並非固定的。已經有計劃要出門旅遊，可以偶爾來網站上查看車票價格，就可以找到特價的車票。

> 瑞典國鐵車票又分可退票、不可退票等。不可退票的車票價格通常比較低，適合行程比較不容易有異動的旅客。若是您不是很確定自己的時間，就購買可退票的車票。

> 在台灣，車票若是沒有使用，或是錯過列車，我們很自然就想到要去退票、換票等。但是在歐洲則不然。若您購買的是不可退票的車票，錯過了，就只能自認了。所以在買訂購車票之前一定要再三確認細節。

🧢 Word Bank

Outward journey	出發行程	Earlier journeys	較早行程
Later journeys	較晚行程	Refundable	可退票
Not available	沒有	Sold out	完售
Included	包含	Reserved seat	保留座
Pre-order	預定		

大人小孩都愛遊樂園

💎 情境對話

Christina: April and I finished the claim report, and I already submitted it to the general manger. With his approval, the report was also forwarded to other departments.

April 跟我完成了客戶報告，我已經將報告交給總經理了。經過總經理的同意，報告也轉傳給其他部門了。

Meredith: Excellent, there won't be any problem during Mr. Grey's visiting. One more thing, did you make the hotel reservation for Mr. Grey? He prefers to stay in the Taipei King 101 Hotel.

很好，Mr.Grey 來訪時就沒有什麼問題了。還有一件事，你幫 Mr.Grey 訂好飯店了嗎？ 他喜歡住在台北 101 國王飯店。

Christina: Yes, I did. Don't worry. We have conducted everything as

有，我訂好了。別擔心，每件事都按計畫安排好

planned. Hey, will you go to Disneyland?

了。嘿，你有要去迪士尼
嗎？

Meredith: We are not sure about it,
why?

還不確定，怎麼了嗎？

Christina: Well, you know the movies "Frozen", it's so popular. Every
girl loves Elsa and Anna, including
my daughter. So, I was wondering if
you could bring her an Elsa doll, if
it's not too much trouble.

你知道「冰雪奇緣」，這
部電影十分受歡迎，所有
的小女生都喜歡 Elsa 跟
Anna.包括我女兒也是。
我想如果不會太麻煩的
話，可以請你幫我帶一個
Elsa 的玩偶嗎？

Meredith: Sure thing. If we go to the
Disneyland in Paris, I can do that.

沒問題，如果我們有去巴
黎的迪士尼，我幫你帶一
個。

Christina Thanks, I really appreciate
it.

真的很謝謝你。

April: Can you bring me a Cambridge Satchel? Please?

那你能幫我買劍橋包嗎？
拜託？

Meredith: Sorry, April. I can't. The

抱歉，April，這我幫不

Part 1 教學篇

Part 2 商品篇

Part 3 旅遊篇

Cambridge Satchel is kind of oversize for my luggage. Elsa is much smaller. We have to travel many places. It would be better if I can keep the luggage **as light as possible**.

上忙。對我的行李箱來說，劍橋包太大了，Elsa 的玩偶小多了。我們要去許多地方，行李越輕越好。

April: Well, you are right. Sorry that I made such an unreasonable request.

你說得很對，抱歉。我的要求太不合理了。

Meredith: <u>Never mind</u>. You can get the Cambridge Satchel online.

沒關係，你在網路上就能買到劍橋包了。

 單字解析

Forward [`fɔrwɚd] *v.* 傳遞
例 Would you forward this letter to his office ?
➡ 你可以將這封信拿去他辦公室嗎？

Oversize [`ovɚ`saɪz] *adj.* 特大的
例 The boy is wearing an oversize jacket.
➡ 那個男孩穿著一件特大號的外套。

句型解析

本書生活化的對話中為您介紹實用的句型或是短句，再舉例句說明，讓您看完之後，就能馬上輕鬆學會，不用背誦!!

As + adj + as possible 盡可能

例 When the light was on, the thief tried to run as fast as possible.

➜ 當燈亮起時，這個小偷盡可能地跑快。

例 The boy is walking as slowly as possible. He doesn't want to go to school.

➜ 那個男生盡可能地慢慢走，他不想上學。

Never mind 沒關係

解 mind 的中文是心智，思想之意。

如 What's on your mind？你的腦袋有什麼？

轉換成通順的中文就是你在想什麼？

Never mind，不要放在心上，就是沒關係的意思。

例 A: I'm sorry to wake you up so early.

B: Never mind. Tell me what's going on.

➜ A: 我很抱歉這麼早把你叫醒

B: 沒關係，告訴我發生什麼事。

以上的單字及短句十分的簡單與實用，

讓您規劃行程之餘，也能自然而然的學習英文哦。

◆ 相關網站

➡ 樂高樂園 Legoland

（圖片來源網址：http://www.legoland.dk/en/）

介紹：小朋友最愛的樂高，在世界各地都有樂高樂園，整個遊樂設施
均為樂高所打造的。絕對讓小朋友眼花撩亂的積木樂園！！

➡ 六旗樂園 Six Flags （圖片來源網址：https://www.sixflags.com/）

介紹：美國著名的遊樂園。適合追求刺激的大朋友，一共有 18 個樂
園，大部分都在美國境內。

➡ 好萊塢環球影城 Universal Studio

（圖片來源網址：http://www.universalstudioshollywood.com）

　　介紹：想見識好萊塢拍片的廠景跟祕密嗎？好萊塢環球影城能一窺究
　　　　　竟，大人小孩都能盡興。有中文網頁介紹。

➡ 日本大阪環球影城 Universal Studios Japan

（圖片來源網址：https://www.usj.co.jp/tw/）

　　介紹：大家最愛去的日本大阪環球影城，有全世界唯一的哈利波特主
　　　　　題館。

➡ **Tivoli** （圖片來源網址：http://www.tivoli.dk/da）

介紹：世界上最早的遊樂園在丹麥。

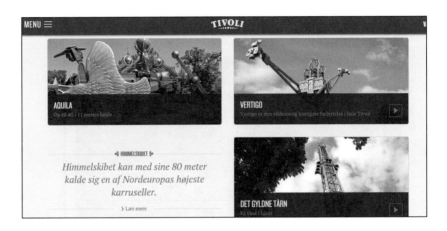

➡ **迪士尼樂園** （圖片來源網址：https://disneyparks.disney.go.com）

介紹：位於佛羅里達的迪士尼樂園，是世界上最大的迪士尼樂園。約
有香港迪士尼的 100 倍面積大小。

 **小貼士**

➤ 歐美的大型樂園園區的範圍非常地遼闊，通常一天是玩不夠的。若可

多規劃幾天，則建議直接入住樂園酒店，並且購買多天的入場票。如此就能玩得盡興。

➢ 隨著美國免簽、歐洲地區免申根簽證，越來越多的旅客喜歡到這些地區旅遊，而其中自由行的旅客也日漸增多。進歐美國家的海關時，會詢問您此行的目的，並要求出示回程機票。千萬不要認為電子機票很方便，而沒有任何的回程紙本證明。請將您所有的行程、來回電子機票、車票等列印出來。進海關時，若碰到官員詢問，就可直接出示。

➢ 在緯度高的國家，有些遊樂園冬天是無法營業的。如丹麥的 Tivoli 樂園。要規劃行程之前，請記得要到樂園官網去查詢相關資料。

🎩 Word Bank

Season Pass	季票	Special offers	特別企劃
Park hour	樂園開放時間	Map	地圖
Ticket	購票	Annual Passports	年度護照

Part 1 教學篇

Part 2 商品篇

Part 3 旅遊篇

情境對話

Meredith: Did you see the news? The Sea World made the announcement that they will cancel a killer-whale show at San Diego theme park in 2016 .

你有看新聞嗎？ 海洋世界發表聲明，2016 年將要取消聖地牙哥的殺人鯨表演。

Christina: I really feel sorry for those animals. They are living creatures, not toys.

我真的覺得那些動物很可憐，牠們是活生生的動物，不是玩具。

April: But everyone loves the killer-whale show. It brings joys and laughes for family.

但是，大家都很喜歡虎鯨的表演，給家人帶來歡笑及快樂。

Christina: Well, if you ever watched

嗯，如果你看過海洋世界

the documentary about how Sea-World train those whales, you would have a different idea.

是如何訓練這些虎鯨的紀錄片，你就不會這樣想了。

April: Really? I haven't heard that before. A documentary?

真的嗎？我沒聽説這件事，有紀錄片？

Christina: Yes, some groups noticed the issues and made the documentary. The Sea World force those whales to archive those unnatural actions. It's against natural, and it's cruel.

有的，有些團體注意到這個問題，並將其拍成紀錄片。海洋世界強迫這些鯨魚完成這種不自然的動作，這是違反動物的天性，很殘忍的。

Meredith: I agree, those controversial, theatrical shows should be forbidden.

説得沒錯。這些充滿爭議、誇張的表演應該要被禁止。

April: I got your point, but everyone loves the Sea World. If there is no sea world park, how can we observe those sea creatures?

我懂你們意思了。但是大家都愛海洋世界，如果沒有海洋世界，我們要去哪裡觀察這些海裡生物。

Christina: Well, if we, the human

如果，我們人類能夠善待

Part 1 教學篇

Part 2 商品篇

Part 3 旅遊篇

being can treat those sea creatures right. It's a good place to show the variety of sea creatures, to learn some knowledge of marine biology. The belief of Sea world is to educate people, not to entertain for visitors.

這些海洋生物。海洋世界便能展現海裡生物的多樣性，我們也能從中學習到海洋生物學。海洋世界的宗旨應該是教育大眾，而不是娛樂遊客。

Meredith: I agree with you. People should **pay more attention to** this issue.

同意你的說法，人們應該多關注這議題。

 ## 單字解析

Controversial [ˌkɑntrəˈvɝʃəl] *adj.* 爭議的

例 Their first meeting was controversial, but finally achieved some agreements.

➜ 他們的首次會議充滿著爭議，但是最後還是達成些協議。

 ## 句型解析

本書生活化的對話中為您介紹實用的句型或是短句，再舉例句說明，讓您看完之後，就能馬上輕鬆學會，不用背誦！！

I got your point 我懂你的意思了

解 Point 當名詞是要點的意思。

I got your point 直譯為我得到你的要點了。

通順的翻譯為:我聽懂你的意思了。

例 A: We can't convene the meeting in such a short notice. Jason can't make it. He is still in Houston.

B: Ok, I got your point. Let's find another day.

➡ A: 在這麼臨時通知之下，我們無法召開會議。Jason 還在 Hoston，他趕不上會議的。

B: 我懂你的意思了，我們再擇日開會。

Pay attention to 對…留意

解 attention 名詞，注意。

Pay attention to + n. 就是對某事留意。

例 You should pay attention to Daryl. He had caused troubles at school.

➡ Daryl 在學校惹了不少麻煩，你要多留意他。

例 No one wants to pay attention to the criminal's complaint. He deserves it.

➡ 沒有人在意那罪犯在抱怨什麼，他是罪有應得的。

以上的單字及短句十分的簡單與實用，
讓您規劃行程之餘，也能自然而然的學習英文哦。

相關網站

➡ 大阪海遊館

（圖片來源：網址 http://www.kaiyukan.com/language/chinese_tradi-tional/）

介紹：有巨大的水族館，親子同遊一天，離大阪影城交通便利。

➡ 沖繩美麗海水族館

（圖片來源：網址 http://oki-churaumi.jp/mm/index.html）

介紹：沖繩著名景點，呈現當地洋流特性及豐富生態，有世界第三大的水槽。

Part 1 教學篇

Part 2 商品篇

Part 3 旅遊篇

➡ 香港海洋公園

（圖片來源：網址 http://www.oceanpark.com.hk ）

介紹：香港不只有購物跟美食，也有海洋公園，擁有全世界最大的水族館圓頂天窗。海洋公園亦結合遊樂園。

➡ 新加坡海底世界 S.E.A. Aquarium

（圖片來源:網址 http://www.rwsentosa.com/Homepag）

介紹：新加坡著名景點，號稱擁有最長的海底隧道。

➡ 美國海洋世界 Sea world park.

（圖片來源：網址 http://seaworldparks.com/en）

介紹：美國海洋世界分布於佛羅里達奧蘭多市、加州聖地牙哥、德州聖安東尼奧市。

➡ 蘇格蘭深海世界 Deep Sea World

（圖片來源：網址 http://www.deepseaworld.com/）

介紹：蘇格蘭的國家級水族館，擁有曾經是世界上最長的海底隧道，有潛水體驗，可和鯊魚一同潛水。

小貼士

➤ 遊樂園這類遊客眾多的旅遊景點，若行程已經確定了，就先上網預購門票，如此可大大地節省您到國外的購票時間。並將門票列印出來，過海關時攜帶。有時候海關除了詢問回程機票之外，還會問旅客的詳細行程。這時，我們就可以將出示門票給海關檢查，證明我們的行程僅是單純的觀光行程，沒有任何非法意圖。

➤ 入海關還有準備一項文件資料-保險，尤其是在歐洲地區。申根地區規定如下: 自 2010 年 10 月 1 日開始，所有須持簽證進入申根國家者都必須提供有效且符合規定之醫療保險證明。此項措施係依據申根簽證條例第十五條，要求所有簽證申請者提供包括緊急醫療救護、緊急醫院治療、醫療遣送或遺體運送等之醫療保險證明，且保險期須涵蓋申請者預計停留於申根會員國境內的期間。所以在您出國之前，請先跟保險公司洽詢，收到保單之後，也將此文件隨身攜帶，以供海關檢查。

Word Bank

Aquarium	水族館	Tickets	購票
Shark dives	鯊魚潛水	Online exclusives 線上獨享優惠	

Part 1 教學篇

Part 2 商品篇

Part 3 旅遊篇

充滿藝術氣息的博物館

💎 情境對話

April: Wow ~ a Chinese billionaire bought a painting for 170 million. That's crazy.

有個中國富商以美金 1.7 億買下了一幅畫。太離譜了。

Christina: I heard that news. The buyer and his wife run an art museum in Shanghai, it called Long Museum. I visited the museum last year.

我聽說過這個消息，買主跟他太太在上海經營一家博物館。叫「龍美術館」，我去年去過。

Meredith: You did? How was it?

你去過？那怎麼樣？

Christina: Very impressive, there are many ancient China articles, the museum still keeps collecting articles from all of the world.

讓人印象深刻，有許多中國古代的藝品，博物館還不斷地在世界各地收集藝術品。

April: <u>Speaking of</u> art collector, I know there is also an enterpriser who collects those art works, Mr.Shi.

說到藝術品的收藏家，我知道有位企業家，許先生也收集藝術品。

Christina: Mr. Shi is not only an enterpriser but also a real artist. He has great passion on classic music and Europe middle ages artwork. He built a museum.

許先生不但是位企業家，也是位藝術家。他對古典音樂跟中古世紀的藝術品十分熱衷。他蓋了間博物館。

Meredith: Last month, we went to the museum. It's so magnificent, and the fountain is splendid. There are many Western art, musical instruments and weaponry collection.

上個月我們去了這間博物館。博物館非常的壯觀，那噴泉更是驚人。有許多西方藝術品、樂器和武器收藏。

Christina: The museum also lends those priceless musical instruments to some brilliant musicians. <u>I would say</u> Mr. Shi's contribution is immeasurable.

博物館還將這些無價的樂器出借給一些有天分的音樂家。我得說許先生的貢獻實在了不起。

Meredith: Indeed, he even donated the museum to the local city.

的確如此，他甚至將博物館捐給了當地政府。

April: Wow ~, now I want to visit the museum.

哇，我想去這博物館看看。

Christina: Well, first you have to make a reservation online.

嗯，你得先在網路上預約。

April: Reservation for a museum?

參觀博物館要預約？

Meredith: Don't complain, it's a method to keep the quality of visiting.

不要抱怨，這是確保參觀品質的做法。

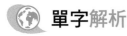 單字解析

Instrument [`ɪnstrəmənt] *n.* 樂器;儀器

例 The kids have to learn a musical instrument at school.

➜ 孩子們在學校必須學習一種樂器。

句型解析

 本書生活化的對話中為您介紹實用的句型或是短句，再舉例句說明，讓您看完之後，就能馬上輕鬆學會，不用背誦 !!

Speaking of 說到…

解 當別人提起某個話題時，我們想要接著這個話題繼續下去時，就能用

Speaking of。

例 A: We went to Denmark last year. It was fun.

B: Speaking of Denmark, it's the world's happiest country.

→ A: 我們去年去丹麥玩，滿好玩的

B: 說到丹麥，這是世界上最幸福的國家。

I would say 我可以這麼說

解 I would say 我可以這麼說，帶有點保證，深信無疑的味道

例 I would say Jason is a very generous person.

→ 我覺得 Jason 是個十分大方的人。

例 I would say that this is the best restaurant in the city.

→ 要我說，這是本市裡最好的餐廳了。

以上的單字及短句十分的簡單與實用，
讓您規劃行程之餘，也能自然而然的學習英文哦。

💎 相關網站

➡ **阿姆斯特丹國家博物館 Rijksmuseum**

（圖片來源：網址 https://www.rijksmuseum.nl）

介紹：建立於 1885 年，超過百年歷史的博物館，本世紀初整修，於
　　　2013 重新開幕。收藏著名的林布蘭的夜巡 night watch。

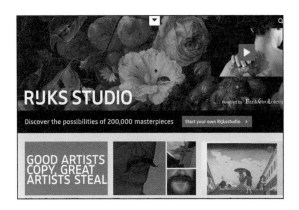

➡ 梵谷博物館 Van Gogh Museum

（圖片來源：網址 http://www.vangoghmuseum.nl/）

介紹：位於荷蘭的梵谷博物館，收藏許多梵谷的畫作，包含著名的向
日葵 Sunflowers。

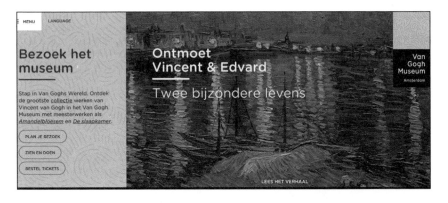

➡ 現代藝術博物館 MOMA Museum of Modern Art

（圖片來源：網址 http://www.moma.org/）

介紹：位於美國紐約，收藏大量的現代藝術。其中還有梵谷著名的星
夜 Starry Night

⇒ **紐約大都會博物館 Metropolitan Museum of Art**

（圖片來源：網址 http://www.metmuseum.org/）

介紹：位於美國紐約，是世界上最大的現代博物館之一。收藏有莫內
　　　的睡蓮池上的拱橋 Bridge over a Pool of Water Lilies

⇒ **大英博物館 British Museum**

（圖片來源：網址 http://www.britishmuseum.org/）

介紹位於英國，是世界上最大的博物館之一，歷史悠久收藏豐富。

Part 1 教學篇

Part 2 商品篇

Part 3 旅遊篇

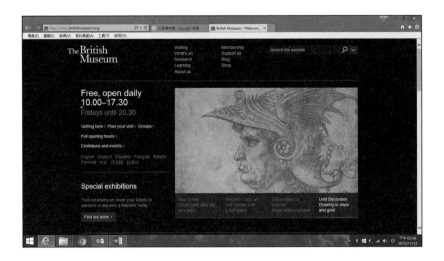

➡ 斯堪森博物館 Skansen Open-Air Museum

（圖片來源：網址 http://www.skansen.se/en/kategori/english）

介紹：博物館一定只有文物嗎？位於瑞典 Skansen Open-Air Museum，為露天博物館。展示早期斯堪地半島居民生活的模式，有建築物、農耕等，還有居民生活在此，模擬早期人們的生活型態。

小貼士

➢ 有的博物館能夠預先預約解說行程，或是現場亦有解說行程。建議您可參加這類博物館所提供的專業解說。能夠讓您對當館的收藏作品能有更深刻的認識，而不光只是走馬看花，湊熱鬧而已。而規模夠大的博物館甚至也有中文嚮導的解說，您可先上網查詢解說時間，再修正您的行程。

➢ 出國旅遊最重要的考量點就是安全。行前請先查訊您要出遊的國家是否有台灣駐地的辦事處，並將其連絡方式隨身攜帶。

➢ 在台灣我們習以為常的便利性，到處都能安心出門。但是在國外，您的行程要預留一些緩衝的時間，不要將行程排得太過緊湊。以免延誤之後的計畫。此外，在規劃行程時，盡量不要排夜晚的活動，尤其是單身女性獨自出遊，務必注意自身安全。

Word Bank

Visiting	參觀	Calendar	日歷
What's on	目前展覽	Artists	藝術家
Research	搜尋	Publication	出版品
Shop	商店	Membership	會員
Explore	探索		

Unit 10 旅遊不忘購物

💎 情境對話

April: Meredith, I just received an e-mail from Mr. Grey, they would like to cancel the Asia trip.

Meredith，我剛收到 Mr. Grey 的信件。他們要取消亞洲的行程。

Meredith: Why?

為什麼呢？

April: Well, there were some acci-dents in their Paris branch office, Mr. Grey has to a flight to Paris tomor-row, In addition, I have already sent the claim investigation report to him. He **is satisfied with** the report and so-lution. Therefore, there is no press-ing need for the Asia trip. He be-lieves that we can handle the

因為他們的巴黎分公司有些意外事件，Mr. Grey 明天就要飛到巴黎去了。此外，我已經將客訴調查報告寄給他了，Mr. Grey 對報告很滿意，也同意我們的處理方法。因此，沒有迫切的理由要到亞洲。他相信我們能夠處

shipping details.

理好裝船的細節。

Meredith: That's good. We should **be more cautious on** next shipping arrangement.

那很好。下次裝船時，我們應該要更加謹慎的。

April: Exactly, Christina and I will go to the factory next week to inspect the loading. We will also take some photos of the shipping cartons and e-mail to Mr. Grey.

說得沒錯。下週裝櫃時，Christina 跟我會去工廠監督。我們也會將出貨的箱子拍照，並將照片傳給 Mr. Grey 看。

Meredith: That's a very comprehensive thought, in this way, we can ensure all details. April, you are a fast learner. I'm glad that you are in our team.

這是很周全的想法，如此一來，我們就能確保所有的細節無誤。April，你學得很快，對我們的團隊幫助很大。

April: Thanks, I'm just doing my best. How is your vacation plan? Have you arranged everything?

謝謝，我只是盡力將事情做好。你的旅遊規劃得如何？一切都安排好了嗎？

Meredith: Yes, we already bought the air ticket, train ticket and booked the hotel, and guess what, we are

是的，機票跟火車票都買好了，飯店也預定好了。而且我們還要去購物中心

going to The Mall.	The Mall.
April: The Mall?	購物中心 The Mall？
Meredith: It's the big outlet shopping center in Italy.	是一個在義大利的 Outlet．

 單字解析

Accident [ˈæksədənt] *n.* 意外

例 There is a car accident in front of the bank, so we should make a detour.

➜ 銀行前面有車禍，所以我們應該繞道而行。

Investigation [ɪnˌvɛstəˈgeʃən] *n.* 調查

例 Kim was involved in a crime investigation.

➜ Kim 被捲入一項犯罪調查。

Pressing [ˈprɛsɪŋ] *adj.* 緊迫的

例 The ISIS is a pressing problem to the whole world.

➜ ISIS 是一項全世界緊迫的問題。

Inspect [ɪnˈspɛkt] *v.* 檢查

例 The custom is inspecting those import containers.

➜ 海關正在檢查這些進口貨櫃。

句型解析

本書生活化的對話中為您介紹實用的句型或是短句，再舉例句說明，讓您看完之後，就能馬上輕鬆學會，不用背誦!!

S + be satisfied with 對什麼…滿意

解 某人對某事滿意，我們用 S+ be satisfied with

例 Jason is satisfied with the result, he finally finished the marathon

➡ Jason 對這結果十分滿意，他終於跑完馬拉松了。

例 Kelly is very satisfied with her new hair style.

➡ Kelly 對她的新髮型很滿意。

S + be cautious on 對……謹慎

例 Kevin is very cautious on children's safety

➡ Kevin 對兒童的安全十分謹慎。

以上的單字及短句十分的簡單與實用，
讓您規劃行程之餘，也能自然而然的學習英文哦。

 相關網站

➡ **Woodburn Premium Outlets**

（圖片來源：網址 http://www.premiumoutlets.com/outlet/woodburn）

介紹：東岸知名 outlets 離紐約大約 1 小時的車程，有超過 220 品牌進駐，甚至連 Chanel 也有暢貨中心。

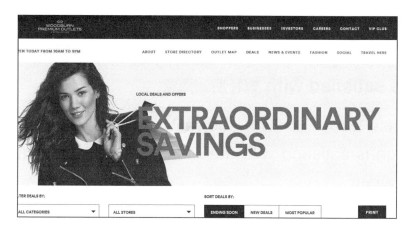

➡ Desert Hills Premium Outlets

（圖片來源：網址 http://www.premiumoutlets.com/outlet）

介紹：西岸知名 outlets 離洛杉磯大約 2.5 小時的車程，有許多一線品牌進駐。

➡ The Mall

（圖片來源:網址 https://www.themall.it/en/outlet-italy/homepage.

html）

介紹：義大利知名 outlets 離佛羅倫斯約 40 分鐘的車程，有接駁 BUS

➡ **Bicester Village**

（圖片來源：網址 http://www.bicestervillage.com/）

介紹：英國知名 outlets 離倫敦約一小時的車程。

➡ 輕井澤王子購物廣場 **Prince Shopping Plaza**

（圖片來源：網址 http://www.karuizawa-psp.jp/web/plazaguide/tw/）

介紹：不想坐長程飛機去歐美？大家最愛的日本，也有好逛的 outlet。東京附近 outlet，有中文網頁，導覽更容易。

➡ 東薈城

（圖片來源：網址 http://www.citygateoutlets.com.hk/shopping/）

介紹：香港知名的名店 outlet 在機場附近。

 小貼士

➢ 逛 Outlet 時一定要多預留時間，因腹地廣大，商品眾多，常常會讓人逛到忘記時間。如果又要辦理退稅的話，常常會等很久。若是錯過接駁車，在郊外的 outlet 坐計程車回來，會是一筆不小的花費哦。

➢ 各地退稅規定不盡相同，可先就要去的商場先查詢清楚。有的直接在商家就可退稅，有的則是先由商家開立退稅單，到機場時再到退稅櫃台集合退稅。若是機場退稅的話，請將您欲退稅的商品集中在一個行李箱裡，因為機場的退稅人員有可能需要核對退稅單及商品是否一致。

 Word Bank

Store Directory	商店指引	Discover	發現
Outlet Map	商場地圖	Guest Service	顧客服務
Luxury	精品	Categories	分類
Brand	品牌	Beauty	美容產品

Part 1 教學篇

Part 2 商品篇

Part 3 旅遊篇

Leader 046

現學現用的 Smart 網購英文

作　　者　Jessica Su
發 行 人　周瑞德
執行總監　齊心瑪
企劃編輯　陳欣慧
執行編輯　陳韋佑
校　　對　編輯部
封面構成　高鍾琪

內頁構成　菩薩蠻數位文化有限公司
印　　製　大亞彩色印刷製版股份有限公司
初　　版　2016 年 6 月
定　　價　新台幣 349 元
出　　版　力得文化
電　　話　(02) 2351-2007
傳　　真　(02) 2351-0887
地　　址　100 台北市中正區福州街 1 號 10 樓之 2
E - m a i l　best.books.service@gmail.com
網　　址　www.bestbookstw.com

港澳地區總經銷　泛華發行代理有限公司
地　　址　香港新界將軍澳工業邨駿昌街 7 號 2 樓
電　　話　(852) 2798-2323
傳　　真　(852) 2796-5471

國家圖書館出版品預行編目資料

現學現用的 Smart 網購英文 / Jessica Su
著. ‒ 初版.-- 臺北市：力得文化,
2016.06 面 ；　公分. -- (Leader ; 46)
ISBN 978-986-92856-5-0(平裝)
 1.商業英文 2.讀本
 805.18　　　　　　　　　105008090